"I'm not an angel. I'm just a person," Starla explained.

Meredith opened her book. "This is the mommy and daddy," she said, pointing to an artist's rendition of a couple in a house with a roaring fireplace. "The daddy has lots of work to do. He comes home too late at night and the mommy and the little kids are sad, 'cause they miss him." She turned a page. "See, they decorate the tree, but the daddy isn't there.

"Then the beautiful angel on top of the Christmas tree hears how sad they are and she comes to life," Meredith continued. "She sprinkles miracle dust on the mommy and daddy. The daddy kisses the mommy under the mistletoe, and then he stays home and opens presents with the kids. See, the angel looks just like you."

The woman glanced over at the white-robed apparition. "Meredith, I'm *not* an angel. How am I going to convince you?"

Meredith just shrugged. The angel lady probably had to keep it a secret in case everybody wanted miracle dust and there wasn't enough!

Dear Reader,

Well, the lazy days of summer are winding to an end, so what better way to celebrate those last long beach afternoons than with a good book? We here at Silhouette Special Edition are always happy to oblige! We begin with *Diamonds and Deceptions* by Marie Ferrarella, the next in our continuity series, THE PARKS EMPIRE. When a mesmerizing man walks into her father's bookstore, sheltered Brooke Moss believes he's her dream come true. But he's about to challenge everything she thought she knew about her own family.

Victoria Pade continues her NORTHBRIDGE NUPTIALS with *Wedding Willies,* in which a runaway bride with an aversion to both small towns and matrimony finds herself falling for both, along with Northbridge's most eligible bachelor! In Patricia Kay's *Man of the Hour,* a woman finds her gratitude to the detective who found her missing child turning quickly to…love. In *Charlie's Angels* by Cheryl St. John, a single father is stymied when his little girl is convinced that finding a new mommy is as simple as having an angel sprinkle him with her "miracle dust"—until he meets the beautiful blonde who drives a rig called "Silver Angel." In *It Takes Three* by Teresa Southwick, a pregnant caterer sets her sights on the handsome single dad who swears his fatherhood days are behind him. Sure they are! And the MEN OF THE CHEROKEE ROSE series by Janis Reams Hudson concludes with *The Cowboy on Her Trail,* in which one night of passion with the man she's always wanted results in a baby on the way. Can marriage be far behind?

Enjoy all six of these wonderful novels, and please do come back next month for six more new selections, only from Silhouette Special Edition.

Gail Chasan
Senior Editor

Charlie's Angels

CHERYL ST.JOHN

Silhouette®
SPECIAL EDITION™
Published by Silhouette Books
America's Publisher of Contemporary Romance

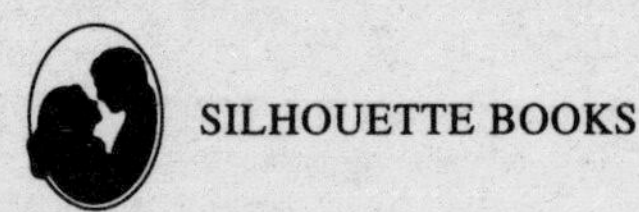

ISBN 0-373-24630-7

CHARLIE'S ANGELS

This edition published by arrangement with Harlequin Books S.A.

Visit Silhouette Books at www.eHarlequin.com

Printed in U.S.A.

Books by Cheryl St.John

Silhouette Special Edition

Nick All Night #1475
Marry Me...Again #1558
Charlie's Angels #1630

Harlequin Historicals

Rain Shadow #212
Heaven Can Wait #240
Land of Dreams #265
Saint or Sinner #288
Badlands Bride #327
The Mistaken Widow #429
Joe's Wife #451
The Doctor's Wife #481
Sweet Annie #548
The Gunslinger's Bride #577
Christmas Gold #627
"Colorado Wife"
The Tenderfoot Bride #679

Silhouette Intimate Moments

A Husband by Any Other Name #756
The Truth About Toby #810

Silhouette Yours Truly

For This Week I Thee Wed

Silhouette Books

Montana Mavericks: Big Sky Brides
"Isabelle"

Montana Mavericks
The Magnificent Seven

CHERYL ST.JOHN

A peacemaker, a romantic, an idealist and a discouraged perfectionist are the words that Cheryl St.John uses to describe herself. The author of both historical and contemporary novels says she's been told that she is painfully honest.

Cheryl admits to being an avid collector who collects everything from dolls to Depression glass, brass candlesticks, old photographs and—most especially—books. She and her husband love to browse antiques and collectibles shops.

She says that knowing her stories bring hope and pleasure to readers is one of the best parts of being a writer. The other wonderful part is being able to set her own schedule and have time to work around her growing family.

Cheryl loves to hear from readers. You can write her at:
P.O. Box 24732, Omaha, NE 68124.

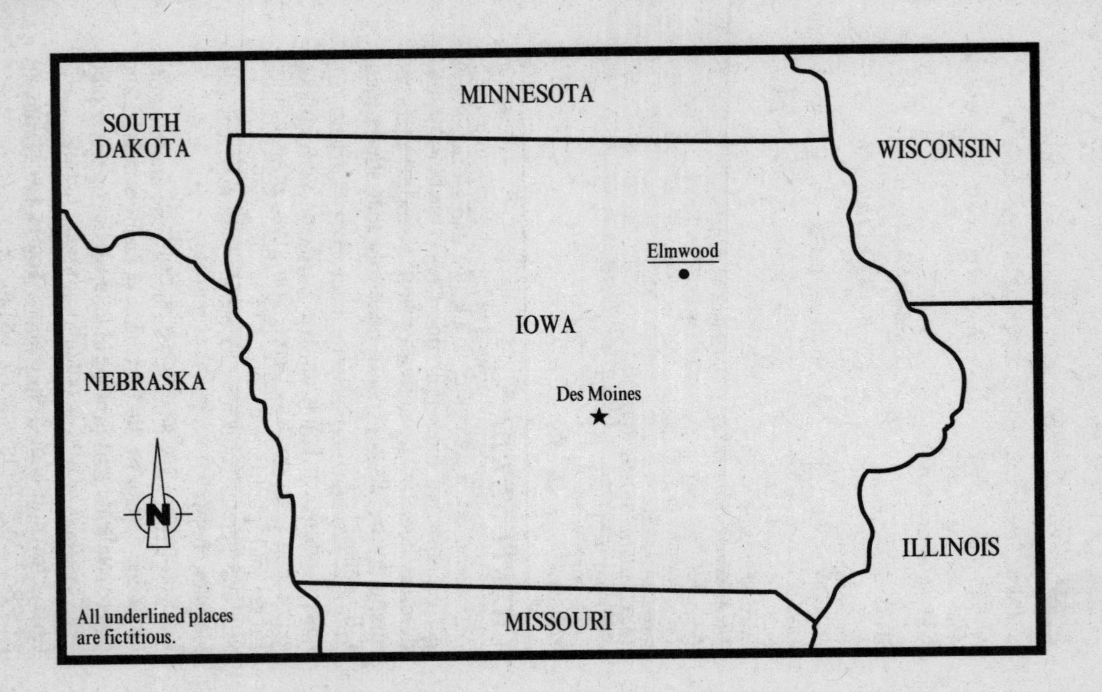

MINNESOTA
SOUTH DAKOTA
WISCONSIN
Elmwood
IOWA
NEBRASKA
Des Moines
N
ILLINOIS
All underlined places are fictitious.
MISSOURI

Chapter One

Christmas was for families. Charlie McGraw glanced around the cheerfully decorated interior of the Waggin' Tongue Grill. A two-foot artificial tree sat at the corner of the counter by the cash register. Lighted garlands had been draped around the window opening that looked into the kitchen, and from the back Harry Ulrich's off-key baritone could be heard humming a tune that switched between "Jingle Bell Rock" and "Yellow Submarine" every other stanza. Finally Charlie's attention wandered to the other patrons.

Snippets of excited conversation drifted his way, making it obvious that Kevin and Lacy Bradford and their two kids had just returned from a shopping trip. Just in time, too, if the snow blowing across the nearly empty parking lot was any indication. Heavy snow had been falling and drifting for most of the day. Charlie wouldn't have brought Meredith out in this weather without his four-wheel-drive Jeep Cherokee.

At another table, Forrest and Natalie Perry took turns picking up a spoon that their chortling baby girl threw onto the floor. Their son, Wade, chattered while finishing off a dish of ice cream. The Perrys lived within walking distance of the Waggin' Tongue.

Charlie glanced at his five-year-old daughter. That morning he'd wrestled her curly dark hair into a fabric-covered elastic band, but strands were trailing down her neck already. He should take her shopping when the weather cleared. Try to get in the holiday spirit. Have her pick out some gifts for her grandparents.

With school closed for two weeks and no kindergarten diversion, Meredith was bored and had taken to following him around his workshop, asking at least ten rapid-fire questions a minute. His responder had been on autopilot most of the morning.

"If a doctor cut open your neck, could he *see* hiccups?" she asked now.

"He could probably see muscles moving or something. I really don't know. I think hiccups come more from your chest."

"If he cut open your chest, then could he see hiccups?"

"Maybe. But a doctor wouldn't do that."

"Where do French fries grow?"

"You cut potatoes into French fries, and potatoes grow in the ground. In Idaho mostly."

"Is Idaho far away?"

"It's in the United States."

She drowned another fry in ketchup. "When are we gonna get a tree, Daddy?"

"Hmm? Oh, soon. We'll get one soon."

"That's what you said the before time, and Christmas is almost here."

Charlie channeled his attention to this last real concern of his daughter's. He leaned over and dabbed a napkin at the corner of her mouth. "I know, honey, but I've had a lot of projects to finish so my customers will get their gifts by Christmas."

She gazed at him with wide blue eyes. "When my mommy was here and I was a baby, did we have a Christmas tree?"

Charlie prepared himself for another endless stream of mommy questions. "Yes, of course we did."

"Did we have a beautiful angel on top of the tree?"

"We have a star for the top, remember? Same one we've always had."

Meredith plopped another dripping fry into her mouth and reached beside her for the book she'd carried everywhere for the past two weeks. He'd picked it up for her at the Dime Store, and she'd insisted he read it to her several times a day.

"We could go over to the library and borrow some new books," he suggested. He knew that one by heart.

"Do they have angel books at the libary?"

"I don't know. We'll have to ask Miss Fenton when we get there. If it's still open. Take a bite of your burger."

Charlie's meal was nearly gone and Meredith was

still munching fries and asking questions. He picked up her hamburger and fed her a bite.

She chewed and swallowed before asking, "Is my mommy a angel now?"

Charlie didn't believe people turned into angels, but he didn't want to destroy any belief that gave his daughter comfort. "What do you think?"

"I think we should find a new mommy for me. You could marry Miss Fenton, Daddy, and she could come live with us."

"Meredith, I barely know Miss Fenton."

"What about my teacher, then, Miss Ecklebe? She's real pretty and she sings nice."

"That's *Mrs.* Ecklebe. She's already married."

Meredith frowned and her rosy lips puckered in displeasure. "Oh."

She'd become obsessed with wanting a mother and talked to him about it incessantly. Though he'd been widowed for several years, Charlie had no desire to find another wife. Just another flaw in his character, perhaps, but he didn't believe true love actually existed, and he couldn't live his life doing things just because other people wanted him to. He'd been down that road before and had no desire to revisit.

Charlie laid his hand on his daughter's dainty shoulder. "We don't really need anyone else. We've got each other."

Her dark lashes swept up and those blue eyes fixed on him as if to say, *Maybe you don't need anyone else, bub.* If she was fifteen, she'd have said, *Yeah, right.*

Why should he feel guilty? That was what this twinge in his chest was, right? No reason for guilt. None whatsoever. A man didn't go in search of a woman just to appease a lonely child. It would be different if he were lonely himself.

Okay, so maybe he was a little lonely. But not enough.

But what would he do when she *was* fifteen? The thought scared him senseless.

He glanced away from Meredith's assessing gaze to the Bradfords. Sure, they looked like the ideal little family: beautiful wife, one girl who looked like her mom, a little guy with a chin like his daddy's, but who knew what went on at home? Or what didn't. True and lasting love only existed in the movies...and then you never actually saw past the credits to what happened when the bills rolled in and disagreements crept up. No, not enough.

Against his better judgment, Charlie glanced at Forrest and Natalie Perry holding hands on top of the table. If he didn't believe that, he'd have to believe it was a flaw in his character; other couples seemed happy.

Meredith's attention turned to the window beside their booth and he followed her gaze. A silver rig with blue detailing pulled into the lot, snow swirling around the cab and trailer as it rolled to a stop. The words *Silver Angel* were emblazoned on the door, a painted pair of wings adorning the *S,* a tilted halo floating above the *A.*

"What's that say?" Meredith's voice was laced with awe.

"Silver Angel," he told her.

She grabbed up her book. "Look! It's just like the halo on my angel book!"

"So it is."

They watched as the driver's door opened and a parka-bundled figure stepped down into the snow and trudged toward the café.

The bell over the door rang.

The driver of the rig stomped snow onto the mat and removed thick gloves, a blast of icy air snaking in and reaching Charlie's ankles.

A slender hand raised to push back the hood of the parka. A shiny waterfall of silver-blond hair spilled across the snow-flecked shoulders of the coat. The ethereally beautiful woman looked like no trucker Charlie had ever seen. Pink tinged her model-perfect cheekbones, and she stuffed the gloves into her pockets before rubbing her hands together.

Meredith inhaled audibly, but Charlie felt as though it had been him. He couldn't seem to fill his lungs, and his chest hurt.

The woman hung her coat on one of the pegs inside the door, revealing a slender shape in long-legged, hip-hugger jeans and a soft-looking pale pink sweater that emphasized her tiny waist. She made her way to the counter, and as she did, every eye in the place was focused on her.

She glanced around, almost self-consciously, nodding a greeting to the families at the tables, before her gaze landed on Charlie and Meredith.

If he didn't take a breath soon, Charlie was going to pass out. He concentrated on breathing in and releasing the air slowly, inconspicuously. He would never admit he'd been waiting for her to look their way.

Her extraordinary eyes were the most translucent blue he'd ever seen, combining with her unusual hair and silver-hued brows for a dazzling prettiness. She smiled and gave them a little wave.

Meredith waved back, delightedly. "Daddy, she's so pretty!"

The young woman turned toward Shirley Rumford who handed her a menu and placed a glass of water in front of her. "What'll ya have, sweetie?"

The vision tucked her hair behind her ear while she looked over the menu, revealing a pearl earring in the lobe of her shell-shaped ear. "Something hot. It's freezing out there. What kind of soup do you have?"

Shirley chanted the short list of soups.

The Perrys called a goodbye to Shirley and left the café, bundling children out into the cold. A few minutes later, the Bradfords paid for their meal and followed. Charlie's gaze was drawn back to the young woman at the counter.

"Daddy, can I go see her up close?" Meredith whispered, none too quietly.

Charlie caught himself staring and turned his attention to the cup of coffee in front of him. "No, it's rude to stare, and we're going to mind our own business."

"But—"

"Meredith, turn around and finish your hamburger so we can go see if the library's open."

His daughter plopped back onto the seat and crossed her arms over her chest. With a dejected pout, she stared at her plate. Five minutes later she still hadn't finished her food.

"You've only taken two bites," he said. "You work on that while I use the rest room and pay our bill."

"Okay." She sighed and picked up the cold hamburger.

Charlie headed back to the rest room.

Meredith sneaked another peek at the angel lady who'd come in from the storm. She was the most prettiest angel ever, even prettier than the treetop angel who came to life in her book.

She flipped open to the page where the angel sprinkles the mommy and daddy with miracle dust and they kiss under the mistletoe. In the picture, all colors of lights twinkled on the beautiful Christmas tree, and three little kids with fuzzy slippers and happy smiles watched from between the stair rails.

If Meredith could get an angel to sprinkle her daddy with miracle dust, he would be happy again. Happy like he used to be. Happy enough to get a new mommy for her, and then they would be a family, just like the family in the book.

Daddy hadn't been happy for a long time.

She tucked the book under her arm, gave the semitrailer a long assessing look and turned her focus back to the angel lady who was paying Miss Rumford for her food.

Meredith had an idea.

* * *

Charlie returned from the rest room to find both red vinyl seats of their booth empty. More than half of Meredith's cold burger sat on her plate. She must have gone into the other rest room.

He sat and observed the snow for a few minutes. Checked his watch. Glanced around the deserted café. Finally he got up and wandered back to the narrow hall that held the rest rooms. Tapping on the door to the women's, he called, "Meredith, you about done in there?"

No reply.

"Meredith? Hello?" Maybe she wasn't in there. He opened the door six inches and called again. "Meredith? Anyone in there?"

Lord, maybe she'd fallen and hurt herself! He shoved the door open and searched the tiny room with two sectioned-off toilets and a sink. Empty. His heart kicked into overdrive.

Spinning on his heel, he hurried back out into the café. The booth where they'd been sitting was still empty. The room was devoid of customers. Shirley was setting napkin-wrapped rolls of silverware on tables. "Shirley, did you see where Meredith went?"

The sixty-something woman looked up from her chore. "I thought she was in the back with you."

"No, she was right here when I went to the men's room."

"I didn't see her, Charlie." Shirley called to the kitchen, "Harry, you seen anything of the McGraw girl?"

Harry and Shirley had owned and run the Waggin' Tongue together for a hundred years, old friends, apparently without romantic involvement, though speculation in Elmwood ran high.

Harry pushed open the swinging door from his domain. "Charlie's little one?"

"Have you seen her?" Charlie asked, real panic lacing his voice now and wrapping his throat tight. He purposefully swallowed the alarm and took a deep, measured breath to keep his thoughts rational.

"Haven't seen anyone. Been in the back room countin' supplies."

Unconvinced until he saw for himself, Charlie pushed past Harry. A few cartons had been stacked here and there; a chain guard and bolt locked the rear door. He inspected the back room, where Harry's grocery list lay on a stool.

"She has to be here somewhere," he said to convince himself, pushing through the swinging door and hurrying to check places he'd obviously missed.

He peered under every table and booth, behind the potted plants. He straightened like a shot. Her puffy pink coat was gone. Turning and staring at the empty seat, his frazzled brain registered what the absence of Meredith's coat meant. "She went outside."

Without bothering to grab his own coat, he sprinted out the front door. She must have tired of waiting for him, or still pouting, had gone out to the Jeep to wait. Maybe she'd been impatient to get to the library.

Fully expecting—*praying*—to find her in the unlocked vehicle, he ran forward and yanked open the passenger side door. His gaze shot to the empty seat…the bare floor. No puffy pink coat. No angel book. No Meredith.

Leaving the door standing open, Charlie stared around the deserted parking lot, the frigid biting wind bringing tears to his eyes, his chest hurting as though someone was standing on it.

Running back toward the café, he studied the ground for footprints. Something caught his eye, and he bent to pick it up. A pink mitten.

Charlie held it while the pressure in his chest built to a painful crush. The area in front of the door was completely trampled, and his own boot prints were plainly visible, though quickly filling with blowing snow. The wind erased any evidence within precious minutes.

Shirley opened the door and called out. "Find her, Charlie?"

He shook his head, trying to make sense of Meredith's disappearance, trying to keep his terror under control so he could think straight and find her.

Harry, bundled in a plaid wool coat, brought Charlie's brown leather jacket out to him. Charlie pulled it on and stuffed the mitten into the pocket. Together they made a circular check of the building and the parking lot, checked the locked car that sat at the corner with a For Sale sign obliterated by snow. They searched beside the ice machine and the cold drink machines and inside the enormous trash container.

"I'd better call the sheriff," Charlie said, his voice as calm as though someone else was speaking. Odd, because on the inside he was screaming his head off and crying like a baby. "And I need to check the library."

Shirley wore a stricken look of concern when they returned and Charlie lunged toward the phone behind the counter. She grabbed Harry's arm and the café owners watched Charlie with eyes round and wide. Nothing like this ever happened in Elmwood. No one had ever been—

Charlie stopped his thoughts dead and punched numbers on the phone. The deputy, Duane Quinn, answered. "This is Charlie McGraw," he managed to say. "My daughter is missing."

Chapter Two

Time had never passed so slowly. Charlie threw up his meal, followed later by the cup of coffee he drank to calm his nerves and wash the taste of fear out of his mouth. The sheriff, Bryce Olson, showed up and made the same search of the premises, coming to the same conclusion: Meredith was nowhere to be found. Bryce jotted notes on an incident report clamped to a clipboard.

"Who else has been in here?" he asked Shirley. The lawman showed genuine concern, which comforted Charlie at the same time it terrified him, because this was all too real.

"The Perrys were here," Shirley told Bryce. "The Bradfords, too. And a lovely young woman trucker. That's it. Weather's keeping people home."

At her mention of the weather, Charlie's alarm intensified. Had Meredith run off into the cold alone? She wouldn't. Would she? She was only five; she didn't know all the dangers.

Had someone taken her out on the treacherous snow-drifted roads? Deliberately *taken her?*

"Let's call the Perrys and the Bradfords," Bryce said. "What about this woman you mentioned? Anything suspicious about her?"

Shirley shook her head. "Had some soup and bought coffee to go."

Charlie knew there were plenty of demented people in the world. He couldn't wrap his mind around the possibility of that beautiful young woman being a part of anything like that. But the television news relayed stories every week about abducted children. He'd heard all those horror stories about teenage girls being drugged and taken away from malls to be sold into prostitution. His stomach contracted again.

Meredith had to be all right, because Charlie didn't know how he could deal with it if she wasn't. If anything happened to his little girl…or if he never knew what became of her…

Stop. Get a grip on yourself. There's a simple explanation. She would turn up and he'd have to decide whether to spank her or hug her first. Even if that woman was part of a kidnapping operation, how would she have known that she'd find a child in this particular out-of-the-way café in a storm? The hand he raised to his forehead was shaking, so he stuffed it into his jacket pocket...where his fingers found the soft material of her mitten.

Panic rose in his throat and he swallowed it down.

Bryce's cell phone rang and he answered it quickly. "Olson. Yeah, Sharon." Sharon was the sheriff's dispatcher, and Bryce listened before he spoke. "Nothing, huh. Okay. Give me numbers for Forrest Perry and Kevin Bradford." A moment later Bryce jotted phone numbers on the edge of his paper. "Okay. Stay put." He disconnected the call.

"Clarey Fenton closed the library early," he told Charlie. "Over an hour ago. Duane checked the streets between here and there. Nothing."

Charlie absorbed the information.

The sheriff called both of the families who'd been in the café and learned nothing, then clipped the phone to his belt. "I'm gonna call the state boys."

Charlie nodded, numbness setting in.

"We should probably even have 'em watch the road for that truck, since it's our only other possibility."

"It had an angel on the side," Charlie said. "The cab was silver with blue detailing, and the logo on the door read *Silver Angel.*"

"Real good, Charlie. That'll give 'em something to go on."

"Maybe she tried to go home," Charlie said suddenly.

"Would Meredith do that?"

"This whole thing doesn't make any sense. I don't know what she'd do. I'd better drive along the road and look."

"I'll get my truck and we can check both sides," Harry said.

It was two miles to Charlie's log home. A long way for a little girl in a snowstorm. A little girl without snow boots or insulated pants. He'd carried her from the house to the Jeep and from the Jeep to the café.

If Meredith was trying to walk, she could easily veer off the road or fall into a ditch.

Charlie got out every fifty feet or so and surveyed the sides of the road and the wooded areas, even calling her name. If she was out here, she might hear him.

But he didn't know. He just didn't know where she might be and that was the worst. A patrol car paused beside him. Duane Quinn rolled down the window. "I'll check up ahead, Charlie. We'll take turns and that way, we'll have the entire road covered. Bryce has organized a search in town."

Charlie nodded, grateful, but desperation and self-reproach were clamping down hard on his control. She'd been bored and lonely, and he'd been putting in long hours at his shop. He could have taken time to go pick out a tree and decorate it—should have, but work dulled the edges of his pain like a narcotic.

He hadn't been there for his child. He'd wasted all those precious hours he should have been spending with her. What would any of that matter if something happened to her?

Duane drove the cruiser on ahead, and Charlie watched the tire tracks fill with snow. His gaze traveled to the bleak, barren trees and white-covered undergrowth. He reached into his pocket and fingered the soft mitten.

Meredith could be anywhere. He pictured her dark hair curling against her neck and the shoulders of her pink coat; remembered those blue eyes, eyes of innocence. His child, so full of life and questions that she bubbled over with energy, could be in serious danger, and he was helpless.

With the thick snow falling around him, blanketing the road and the countryside with silence, Charlie gazed heavenward…and prayed.

"'You've got a way with me. Somehow you got me to believe…in everything that I could be….'" Starla Richards sang along with her *Notting Hill* CD, the coffee she'd been nursing giving her the energy she'd needed. She glanced at the digital clock on the dash. About another six hours to Nashville, unless the storm got worse. Hopefully, the farther south she went, she'd drive out of it.

The windshield wipers kept the snow out of her line of vision, but packed it at the bottom of the windshield and occasionally stuck to the wipers in a squeaky blob that ricocheted to and fro before finally knocking itself loose.

"'I gotta say, you really got a way…'"

Not exactly how she'd planned to spend the week before Christmas. She should be trying out her lobster gumbo recipe and watering the Christmas tree in her apartment back home in Maine. The grand opening of her restaurant was scheduled two weeks from now and she had plenty of preparations left. But as luck would have it, her dad had broken his leg and landed himself in traction just when this load needed delivery in time for a juicy bonus.

It had been nearly three years since she'd driven a load, two and a half of those years spent in culinary arts school, finishing her degree. Starla hadn't wanted any part of the road again. Not for any reason.

But this was different. Her dad needed help with the only other thing besides her that meant anything to him, the only thing he'd wanted since her mother had died—this rig. And she hadn't been able to refuse running the load. She'd grown up on the road, eaten in greasy-spoon restaurants and showered in concrete-block stalls since she was thirteen. It wasn't like she didn't know what to do, how to drive, keep the log sheets, make the safety checks. She'd fallen right back into the routine as though she'd never been away.

This truck was much nicer than the one they'd shared all those years. The *Silver Angel* was her dad's dream rig.

She would call him in another half hour, just before his neighbor brought him supper, because he would be watching the weather channel and charting her progress. Humming, she plugged her cell phone into the charger and made sure the green light came on.

A soft sound distracted her and she turned down the stereo volume to listen. Nothing coming from the engine. She checked the side mirrors and the road behind her and, once satisfied that it had been nothing, she turned the music back up.

A sound came again. Louder this time, and unmistakably from the sleeper area behind her. Heart lurching, she cautiously leaned to the glove box and pulled out her dad's revolver. It could be an animal. A cat or a raccoon might have slipped in while she'd been doing her log check. How many times had her dad cautioned her to close the door after grabbing the clipboard?

Starla scanned the white-blanketed vista ahead and behind, then guided the rig off to the side of the road and put the transmission in Park, at the same time unfastening her seat belt.

Jabbing the power button on the stereo, she plunged the cab into silence and turned sideways in the seat to get up. Crouched beneath the head liner, she stepped to the doorway and flipped on the overhead light. There was room to stand straight in the sleeper and she moved forward.

A bundle of bunched covers in the corner of the bed rustled. The hump was bigger than a cat or a raccoon. Heart hammering, she swallowed hard and pointed the gun. "What are you doing back here?"

The covers moved again. Not really a big enough lump to be a person—unless it was a very small person. Keeping the revolver at the steady in her right hand, she leaned forward and, with her left, jerked the blankets away.

She saw a tumble of dark hair first, followed by a small white face and blue eyes. A child!

Quickly Starla jammed the revolver into a storage cabinet overhead and bent to the little girl. "What are you doing here? How did you get in? Who are you?"

The child's lower lip quivered, and her gaze moved to the cabinet above and back to Starla. "I'm Meredith."

Completely confused, but relieved that her intruder was harmless, Starla sat on the edge of the bunk. "What are you doing in my truck?"

The girl sat up swiftly, all signs of worry erased, and crossed her stockinged legs. She wore a red jumper with a *Sesame Street* character on the bib. Grover, maybe. No, Elmo, that was the red one. "You have to help my daddy."

Knowing full well there was no one else hiding in this cramped space, Starla looked around, anyway. "Where's your daddy? What's wrong with him?"

"He's at home. And he's sad. That's why you have to help. If you sprinkle some of your miracle dust on him so he can be happy again, I know he'll find me a new mommy."

Starla rubbed her brow in confusion. "Where is home?"

Meredith shrugged.

Starla pressed, "Where do you live?"

"In a brown house."

Oh, my goodness. Placing her hands on her knees and biting her lip, Starla concentrated. Couldn't be too hard to figure out where the kid had come from. The last place she'd stopped had been that café back on the highway a while back.

Of course. The pieces of mental puzzle slipped into place. This child had been seated at a booth with her father. Everyone in the place had stared at the stranger, the lady truck driver, but this little girl had waved and looked happy to see her. "Do I look like somebody you know?"

Meredith nodded happily.

"Who? Your mommy?"

The child frowned then and shook her head.

"Who do I look like?"

"You're the angel, like the one in my book." She pointed to the colorful cover. "See?"

"I'm not an angel," Starla denied, glancing at the picture of the platinum-haired celestial being. "I'm just a person."

Meredith shook her head. "Says you're a angel right on the door of this truck, don't it?"

"That's just the name of the truck. Men are silly like that. They name things. Like trucks. My dad calls his truck *Silver Angel*."

"You're the angel," the child insisted, pointing. "This one." She opened the book and turned pages until she came to a picture of the woman sprinkling sparkly dust. There was a smear that appeared to be ketchup across the corner of the page. "See right here?" Meredith turned enormous blue eyes on her. "My daddy needs some of your miracle dust. Please say you'll help him."

"That's just a story," Starla told her. "It's pretend. If I was an angel, what would I be doing driving a truck across Iowa in a snowstorm?"

Not to be dissuaded from her cause, Meredith ignored the denials and used five-year-old logic to explain, "Aunt Edna who lives at the nursey home said she was in a car crash once, and a beautiful angel in a white robe sat right on the seat beside her and kept her from going off a bridge."

"Your aunt Edna is in a nursing home?"

"She's not my aunt. That's just her name. She's prob'ly somebody's aunt, though."

"Well, as you can see," Starla replied, gesturing to her cashmere V-neck sweater and jeans, "I don't have a white robe."

"Uh-huh." Meredith nodded and pointed to where Starla's white satin dressing gown and pajamas hung on a plastic hook.

"Those are my pajamas." Starla shook her head in negation. Or was it confusion? "How did you get in here?"

"I watched when Miss Rumford carried dishes to the back. When you got your coat, I followed. I was behind the gas pumper and saw you take your papers from inside and walk around, looking at the tires and the lights and stuff. You left the door open."

She certainly had. After all Dad's warnings.

Meredith scooted toward the edge of the bed. "I have to go potty."

Starla held her forehead in her hands, her mind thrown into overdrive. She would have to take this child back to her parents. To her father. To that café. She was going to lose...her gaze shot to her watch...nearly *three hours*, even if she made good time!

The child's family would be frantic by now.

"Meredith," she said suddenly. "We have to let somebody know that you're okay."

"Daddy's going to be mad. Really mad."

"I'm sure he's more worried than mad."

"I *really* have to go potty."

Ten minutes later, after showing Meredith the camper-size toilet, digging a bag of popcorn from a supply cupboard, then buckling her into the seat belt on the passenger side, Starla asked. "Do you know your phone number?"

Meredith nodded and reeled off the number. Starla jotted it on the edge of a log sheet on her clipboard and unplugged her phone to dial. She got an answering machine. "He's not there."

Of course he wasn't there. He was either at the café or at the sheriff's department, reporting a missing child.

"He gots a cell phone, too," Meredith told her.

"Oh! Do you know that number?"

Meredith shook her head.

"That's okay. I'll call information for the café. What's it called?"

"Miss Rumford's restaurant?"

"Yes, what's the name of it."

"Miss Rumford's restaurant."

"Of course." Starla called long distance information and asked for the café in Elmwood, Iowa. She jotted another number down and called it.

"Waggin' Tongue," a male voice said.

"Oh, hi. Um, is there a man there who is looking for his daughter?"

"Charlie! It's for you!"

At the man's shout, Starla jerked the phone away from her ear, then returned it tentatively. "Hello?"

"Hello!" a man said into the phone. "This is Charlie McGraw."

"I don't quite know how to say this," she began. "I have your daughter with me—"

"Oh God," he said. "What do you want? Is she all right?"

"She's fine, she's just fine. I…I don't want anything."

"Please don't hurt her. Let me talk to her!"

Starla held out the phone. "Meredith, tell your father that you're all right."

Meredith sank back against the seat and shook her head, her chin lowered to her chest.

"Just say you're okay, so he knows. He's worried about you."

Meredith shook her head, and her lower lip protruded enough to park a truck on it.

"She's afraid," Starla began to explain, talking into the receiver.

"What's wrong? What have you done with her? Where are you?"

"I haven't done anything! She thinks you're mad at her. We're on I-80, almost to Rock Island. I just discovered her in my sleeper about fifteen minutes ago."

"Discovered her? What do you mean?"

"Well, she's a…a stowaway."

"You're telling me she got into your truck all by herself?"

"Apparently. She keeps calling me the angel lady and asking me to sprinkle you with miracle dust."

An audible groan came from the other end of the line.

"I've tried to explain that I don't have any special powers, but she's convinced I can do something she wants me to do."

"Put the phone to her ear, will you, please?"

Starla reached out and placed the phone to the little girl's ear. "You've got her."

Meredith's wide blue eyes accused Starla for a moment, then she turned her gaze away while she listened. She gave a half nod, caught her lower lip between her teeth. A tear formed at the corner of her eye. "I love you with my whole heart, too, Daddy," she said finally. "I will. Okay. I will."

She looked at Meredith. "He wants to talk to you."

"I'm really sorry about this," the man said to her. "And I'm sorry I yelled at you. I've been out of my head with worry."

"I can imagine."

"Look, I can come get her."

Starla glanced at the clock on the dash. "No, I'll bring her back. I'd rather do that than sit here and wait. We'll be there in an hour and a half or so."

"The weather's getting worse," he said. "Take your time."

"I'll drive carefully. I have to find a place to turn around." It was easy for him to tell her to take her time.

She was the one losing precious hours needed to deliver her load on schedule. They exchanged cell phone numbers and he told her to let Meredith call him if she wanted and he'd pay for the charges.

Starla buckled in, pulled out onto the pavement and watched for an Exit sign.

"Can we listen to your music some more?" Meredith asked.

Starla flipped on the CD player, and music filled the cab.

"Is this angel music?"

"Nope. It's a soundtrack."

"Oh. Some angels don't have wings that show, isn't that right?"

The windshield wipers cleared two arcs and Starla peered into the driving snow and spotted the green sign indicating an exit. "I wouldn't really know about that."

Within minutes they were headed back the other direction.

"Do you know my mommy?"

Starla kept her attention on the white blur of road and sky. "I don't think so. I don't know anyone in Elmwood."

"No, my mommy's in heaven. She's a angel, too."

She absorbed that information with equal measures of understanding and sympathy. "Meredith, I'm not an angel. I'm just a person. I was a baby once and I went to school, just like you."

The child straightened in her seat, settled the book squarely on her lap and opened it. "This is the mommy and daddy," she explained, pointing to an artist's rendition of a couple in a house with a roaring fireplace. "The daddy has lots of work to do, and he goes to his job with his beefcase."

"Mmm-hmm."

"He comes home too late at night and the mommy and the little kids are sad, 'cause they miss him." She turned a page. "See they make cookies, but the daddy isn't there. And they decorate the tree, but the daddy isn't there."

Starla was listening, but her concentration was on her driving.

"Then, the beautiful angel on the top of the Christmas tree hears how sad they are and she comes to life. See, she looks just like you."

Starla glanced over at the white-robed apparition. Pale blond hair would be a comparison, she supposed.

"She sprinkles miracle dust on the mommy and daddy. The daddy comes home and kisses the mommy under the mistletoe, and then he stays home and opens presents with the kids. Isn't that a nice story?"

"Very nice. What do you like the most about the story?"

"That there's a mommy and a daddy. Two of them."

The yearning in the child's voice was plain. "Sometimes a daddy is enough," Starla said. "Especially if he loves you as much as a mommy and daddy put together. That's how much my dad loves me."

Meredith picked up on that right away. "Is your mommy a angel, too?"

"She died when I was twelve. I was older than you, but I still had only a dad for a lot of years. He taught me to drive a truck."

"He did? What else?"

"He taught me how to load and fire a weapon. He made me go to a martial arts school."

"What's that?"

"That's where they teach you to protect yourself."

"Oh. Can you flip guys and stuff, like the Power Puff Girls?"

"Nothing that fancy," she replied.

"But you're a angel, can't you just zap bad people?"

"Meredith, I'm *not* an angel. How am I going to convince you?"

Meredith shrugged.

The questions continued until Starla asked Meredith to read the book to her again. The child tired and fell asleep for about half an hour, then woke groggy. "Where are we?"

"We're almost there."

"Can I call my daddy?"

Starla punched the numbers and handed her the phone. "Tell him we're on the highway, not far away now."

"Hi, Daddy...he wants to talk to you."

"Hello," Starla said into the phone.

"They're closing the highway and the interstate," he told her.

Her heart sank. She would be trapped. "Great."

Ice was pelting the windshield and freezing now. She had slowed to a crawl and could barely see. The sun had set long ago, and the darkness was lit by the snow and her two beams of headlights that were growing dimmer by the minute. "Sleet must be freezing to my headlights. I can barely see in front of the hood."

"Can you make out any landmarks?"

"Not really. Wait, there's a sign up ahead. It's covered with snow, I can't tell. I think it's the Elmwood sign."

"You're only a quarter mile from my place if it is," he told her.

"Okay, I'm watching. It's slow going."

"That's okay. You'll see a grove of trees on your left."

"I'm passing them now."

"Look up ahead to the right now. Go slow around the curve."

"I'm going slow."

"I'm in a Cherokee at the end of my drive with my headlights on. Can you see anything?"

She couldn't. "No…no…wait, we're sliding!" Starla dropped the phone to grab the wheel with both hands and guide the rig around the curve. She felt the trailer slide, jackknifing toward her. Momentum and treacherous ice jerked the wheel out of her control, sending the cab toward the ditch.

Grabbing Meredith's pink coat, she flung it over the child's head and held it there to protect her as the truck slid sideways. An enormous jerk knocked her against the door, and pain wracked the side of her head. Starla's vision faded to blackness.

Chapter Three

Through the falling snow and the darkness, Charlie made out the headlights as they veered abruptly. He held the phone to his ear and shouted: "Hello! Hello!"

His daughter's crying could be heard, a sound that terrified and assured him at the same time. "Meredith?"

He threw the Jeep into low gear and guided it slowly and carefully onto what he hoped was the pavement. The four-wheel drive pulled the vehicle through the buildup of snow, but would do precious little if he hit a patch of ice like that truck had, so he crept forward slowly. He couldn't see where the road was supposed to be, and the phone poles on the other side of the ditch gave him pathetic guidance. As long as he didn't get too close to those, he should stay on the road.

"Daddy?"

"Meredith, are you all right?"

"Da-addy!"

Her sobs tore at his already overworked heart.

"Meredith, talk to Daddy. Are you all right?"

"Uh-huh."

"And the lady? Is she all right?"

"She covered my head with my coat, so I couldn't see nothing. I'm scared!"

"I'm on my way, baby. I'm almost there."

"Hurry, Daddy!"

"It's okay, sweetie. Can you see the lady?"

"Uh-huh."

Charlie was afraid to ask anything more. How would Meredith know if the woman was alive or dead, and what difference could she make in either case?

"She gots blood on her head," she volunteered finally, then whimpered.

Oh, Lord. "Okay, I'm almost there."

He could see the headlights clearly now. The semi had slid from the road and was in the shallow ditch, right side up, thank goodness. Charlie parked on what he hoped was the side of the road and got out, plunging into snow halfway up his calves to make his way down the bank to the cab. The truck engine thrummed, loud in the snow-silent night.

He got to the door and found it locked. He pounded on the metal. "Meredith! You have to unlock the door!"

A moment later a sound indicated she'd found a power lock. He yanked open the door to hear her terrified cries. Unfastening the seat belt, and pulling himself up, he scooped her into his embrace and comforted her, running his hands over her head and limbs. She seemed perfectly unharmed.

The driver, however—the beautiful young woman with the silver mane of hair, sat slumped toward them, her seat belt fastened across her breasts, a crimson rivulet streaming from a gash on her forehead, down her temple, a stain spreading on the shoulder of her pink sweater.

"Meredith, I'm going to take you to the Jeep and come back for her." Hurriedly, he shoved the child's arms into her pink coat, carried her up the incline and deposited her in the back seat. "Put your seat belt on. I'll be right back."

Wide-eyed and hiccuping from her recent near-hysterical crying, the child nodded her acquiescence.

Charlie opened the rear of the Jeep, took out an old plaid blanket, and plowed his way back down the bank. He paused to scoop a gloveful of snow, then, once inside the cab, he turned off the engine and dabbed the snow on the woman's forehead. She had a cut about an inch long that looked fairly deep. He stuffed the keys in his pocket and unbuckled her. After wrapping the blanket around her, he slid her out of the cab as gently as he could and struggled up the bank with her held in his arms. He slipped to his knees twice, but retained his hold on her.

He was sweating by the time he got her into the back of the Jeep, covered her wound with a fresh blob of snow, tied it with his wool scarf and closed up the back.

Fearful of backing off the edge of the road if he tried

to turn around, he carefully backed the Jeep along on the highway until he was certain the access area he reached was wide enough to back into and head out going forward. Perspiration cooled his forehead as he got the vehicle turned around and drove toward home. He would never make it to the town's clinic in this weather without another accident. He couldn't see the road. Meredith was uncharacteristically silent, a blessing, because the hazardous trip took all his concentration.

He had no idea how badly the woman was hurt, or if he'd done her more damage by moving her, but he didn't think so. She'd been wearing her seat belt; her head had probably hit the steering wheel or the side window.

Grabbing his phone, he called the sheriff's office. Sharon, the dispatcher answered. "I have Meredith," he said. "She seems fine. But the truck the woman was driving slid off the road and the driver's unconscious. She has a pretty bad cut on her forehead. I have her with me, but I can't make it to town."

"Where are you?"

"I'll be at my place in a few minutes."

"Okay. I'll let Bryce know and I'll call Dr. Kline. He can use Sheigh Addison's snowmobile and come out to your place."

"I'm almost there." Charlie hung up and focused on getting the Jeep onto his property. Once he hit his drive, there were no more drainage ditches to fear. He found the path and drove along the length of gravel, clear to the front of his garage where he used the remote to open the door. He pulled into the safe dry garage and breathed a sigh of relief.

After getting Meredith out of the back seat and placing her inside the house, Charlie went back for the young woman. He carried her through the mudroom, across the kitchen and into the great room where he laid her on the leather sofa. After hurriedly running back and hitting the button to close the garage door, he turned on indoor lights and checked her head.

The snow had helped to slow the flow of blood from the wound. He grabbed clean kitchen towels and applied pressure to the cut. Meredith stood nearby, her eyes wide with fright, her dark hair curling wildly around her stricken face.

Charlie reached for her with one arm, and she flung herself against him. He sat on the floor beside the sofa to hold his baby and keep pressure on the woman's cut.

He'd never been so frightened in his entire life. Almost losing this child had been a gruesome experience. He hugged her warm little body close, felt her trembling and inhaled the wonderful child scent he so loved. His heart couldn't contain his gratitude at having her safe in his embrace. His eyes stung.

"Are you so, so mad, Daddy?" she asked in a tiny voice.

"We'll talk about that later. Not right now." He kissed her hair, her soft cheeks. Closed his eyes and thanked God with his whole being.

They were still sitting like that when he saw a headlight flicker across the lawn and heard the rumble of the snowmobile's engine cut. "Why don't you go to your room and rest on your bed for a little while?" he said to his daughter.

Obediently she got up and headed for the hallway.

Charlie let Garreth Kline in. "She's right here." He led the young doctor to the sofa.

"What's her name?" the tall dark-haired man asked.

Charlie realized he didn't know and told him so.

Garreth took a penlight and raised one of the woman's eyelids at a time. "Her pupils are equal and reactive." He removed the cloth to examine the cut. "This needs a couple of stitches. Miss? Can you hear me? Miss?"

"What's wrong with her?"

"Knocked out, I'd say. Took a good whack on the head there."

"Are those medical terms?"

Garreth ignored him and rubbed his knuckles against her sternum. "Can you wake up and look at me?"

Her eyelids fluttered open.

"Hi. I'm a doctor. Do you know your name?"

She frowned, but she said softly, "Starla."

"Good. Starla, you have a cut on your head. I'm going to numb the area first, and then I'll suture it."

She nodded and closed her eyes.

The doctor tugged on latex gloves and prepared a syringe. Charlie washed his hands in case Garreth needed his help, but then just stood by as Garreth neatly closed the wound, tied a knot and clipped the thread. "She's going to have a whopping headache," the doc said, removing the gloves and placing supplies back in his bag. "Do you have any Tylenol?"

Charlie found a bottle.

"She should rest, in case she has a concussion. If she falls asleep and isn't responsive, or if she vomits, call me."

"What am I going to do with her?" Charlie asked.

"Just keep her comfortable. And don't let her drive."

Charlie shook his head. "Funny."

Garreth shrugged. "Seriously. Looks like you've got yourself a house guest for the duration of the storm."

Charlie studied the woman on his sofa, then looked at Garreth, whose eyes held a twinkle.

"The situation doesn't look all that bad, Charlie."

"I just had one of the worst scares of my life. I need some time to recover."

"Meredith's okay? Should I have a look at her?"

"I'd appreciate that, thanks." He led the way to his daughter's room. "Look, honey, Dr. Kline is here."

Meredith sat up on her bed, a worn blue bunny hugged to her chest. "Is the angel lady okay?"

"She's fine," Garreth told her. "She just got a bump on the head and a cut. How about you? Did you bump your head?"

Meredith said no. "The angel lady covered my head up with my coat. I was scared."

"She was protecting you, you know that, right?"

Meredith nodded. "That's what angels do. That's what Aunt Edna's angel did. Protected her from a car crash."

Charlie exchanged a look with the young doctor. Janet Carter's aunt would tell the story of the angel in the car to anyone who would listen, and anyone who'd ever met her had heard the tale. What that old lady's story and his daughter's experience today had in common, he couldn't imagine, but Meredith had found a comparison. Confirmation of her theory, apparently.

With his penlight, Garreth checked Meredith's pupils. He felt her arms and legs and pushed lightly on her chest and her stomach. She seemed to have no pain anywhere. "Looks like you came through without a scratch," he said to her.

She nodded gravely. "But my daddy's mad."

"I'm sure he's more glad to see you safe than he is mad."

She gave her father the resigned look of a condemned prisoner. "We're gonna talk 'bout it later."

"Well, I'll leave you to that," Garreth said, straightening and heading into the other room.

Charlie followed him. "Thanks for coming."

"Your lady vet's snowmobile has come in handy more than once."

"I had dinner with her once, she's hardly *my* lady vet."

Garreth only shrugged. He made his way back to the patient. "I'm leaving now, Starla. Charlie is going to watch out for you. You're in good hands. If you need anything, he'll call me."

She opened her eyes and nodded.

Garreth pulled on his coat and gloves. "Call if you need me."

Charlie closed the door behind him. Slowly he made his way back to the exquisite woman on his sofa. She was here because of his daughter. Had been injured returning his precious Meredith. "I'm really sorry about this," he said.

Her lids raised and she focused those unusual blue eyes on him. Something in his chest fluttered. "That's okay."

"Do you have a headache?" he asked.

She licked her lips. "Either that or there's a little guy with a jackhammer inside my skull."

"The doc said you could have some Tylenol. I'll get it for you."

"Thanks."

He went for water, shook a couple of capsules out of the bottle and secured the childproof lid.

"How's Meredith?" she asked.

"She's just fine."

"She didn't get any bumps?"

"No."

"What about the truck?" Her eyes held grave concern.

"In the ditch. Snow up to the wheel wells. It's not going anywhere."

"I was afraid of that. Was it still running?"

"Yes, I shut it off and took the keys?"

"Did you lock it?"

"I don't think so. It's not going anywhere, and the roads are closed. Nobody's going to be on that highway."

She tried to sit up. "Oh, boy, I'm dizzy."

Charlie knelt beside her and reached an arm behind her back to help her sit. He had to help her hold the glass, too, because her hand was shaky. She smelled like a blend of powder and spice, exotic and feminine, and her fingers beneath his were slender and soft. He experienced the same trouble breathing that he had in the restaurant when he'd first seen her.

He lowered her back to a lying position. "I'll get you some pillows and covers," he told her. When he returned, he went to the end of the sofa. "Can I take your boots off?"

She raised one foot.

He reached inside her pant leg and unzipped, then tugged and the black leather boot came off, revealing a slender foot in an ordinary white sock. The sight gave him a hard-on so quickly, he almost turned away. Instead he unzipped and removed the other boot, opened the blanket and covered up the sight of her feet and her legs and her hips in those low-cut jeans and...

The shoulder of her pink sweater was soaked with blood. "I'm going to get you a clean shirt. I'll bring a pan of water and a cloth. You can clean up and change. Can you do that?"

She glanced down at her sweater. "Sure. I didn't get blood on your furniture or carpet or anything, did I?"

"No. You may have some inside the cab of your truck, though. I don't really remember. I was in a hurry to get you both out."

He found the smallest sweatshirt he owned, which

happened to be a faded gray and emblazoned with Iowa Hawkeyes, filled a pan with warm water and suds and handed her a washcloth. "I'll be in the other room. Call if you need me."

He helped her sit up and left.

Meredith would be getting hungry. He should think about finding something to eat. He opened a cupboard and listened to the sound of water splashing behind him.

"I don't know if this stain will come out," she called. "Would you mind soaking it?"

"I'll give it a shot. Looks like a nice sweater."

"My dad gave it to me. He likes me in pink."

He doubted there was a color of the rainbow she didn't look good wearing. She was probably even more appealing in nothing at all.

Closing the cupboard, he opened the refrigerator and stared inside. Why had he thought *that*? He was going to be cooped up with her for the time being; he'd better control his thoughts—and his hormones.

"Your name's Charlie?" she called.

"Yeah."

"Charlie, I'm finished."

He went to get the sweater, warm from her body, and the pan of sudsy water. She swam in his gray sweatshirt, and had pushed the sleeves up to reveal slender forearms.

Back in the kitchen, Charlie used the same pan to fill with cold water and soak her sweater. First he rinsed the soft fabric under the faucet until the water stopped running pink, then he plunged it down in the water.

"Add a little salt," she called.

"Salt?"

"It's supposed to help take out blood stains. I read that somewhere."

"Okay." He poured a teaspoon in and swished it around. Martha Stewart, he wasn't.

Meredith appeared in the kitchen doorway. "Can I talk to the angel lady now?"

"Her name is Starla. Can you call her that, please? And while you're at it, maybe you should tell her you're sorry for making her come back here in a snowstorm."

"Okay, Daddy."

He dried his hands and stepped to the doorway. Meredith crossed the living room and paused beside the sofa.

Starla's blond head moved as she turned to look at the little girl. "Hi," Starla said. "How are you?"

"I'm okay. Did the doctor do that to you?" Meredith pointed to Starla's forehead.

"Yes. Does it look pretty bad?"

Meredith nodded. "Does it hurt?"

"No, he gave me a shot of novocaine before he stitched it. Do you think I'll be able to play the violin after they take out the stitches?"

Meredith eyes widened. "I don't know. Daddy?"

Charlie chuckled and joined them, sitting on a chair. "It's an old joke, honey. I'll bet Starla didn't play the violin before she hit her head."

"Were you tricking me?" Meredith asked.

"Yes, I was." Starla turned her attention to Charlie. "You didn't happen to grab my phone, did you?"

He shook his head.

"I need to call my dad. He's expecting to hear from me, and he'll be worried, especially if he calls and my phone just rings and rings."

"No problem." Charlie grabbed the cordless phone from the counter between the kitchen and living room and handed it to her. "Use mine."

"It's long distance," she warned.

"And you're here because of me," he replied in the same tone.

She took the phone and punched in numbers.

"Come on, Meredith, I'll fix a snack."

"But I didn't getta say it yet."

"Say it after she makes her call."

She followed him to the kitchen.

For once when he would have welcomed Meredith's chatter to cover the conversation in the other room, the child remained silent. Bits of Starla's side of the conversation floated to them as she explained what happened. "I swear, I'm all right… I know…well, I don't know…how long it will be before they can get here to pull it up… The highway's closed, anyway… I'm so sorry…make it up some other way. Maybe if I call… I know what this meant to you… Yes, I'm perfectly fine…yes, it's just a truck…some other way… Daddy…."

Charlie got the impression that something more than a few days' travel was at stake. Was she in some kind of trouble?

He put together grilled cheese sandwiches and

mugs of hot tomato soup, and carried a tray into the other room.

Starla sat up, but she only took a few bites. She sipped the cup of tea he brought her, then nestled back down into the covers.

"Starla?" Meredith said timidly.

"Yes?"

"I'm sorry I got in your truck and made you get in a accident."

"The accident wasn't your fault, honey. They call them accidents because they're nobody's fault."

Meredith didn't seem reassured by those words, but Charlie stayed out of the dialogue.

"It's okay," Starla said, somehow understanding the child needed forgiveness. "I'm not mad at you."

Meredith nodded. "Okay."

Meredith picked at her food and Starla drifted into sleep. After cleaning up their dishes, Charlie held his daughter on his lap.

"It's time to talk now," he told her.

She nodded gravely and raised innocent wide eyes that immediately filled with tears. "I did a naughty thing, huh, Daddy?"

"Yes, you did. It was a dangerous thing. There are rules about strangers and about going anywhere by yourself, and the rules are to keep you safe. Do you understand?"

She nodded. To her credit, she didn't use an excuse. "I'm very, very sorry."

"What do you think is a fair punishment?"

They'd had similar conversations in the past, so she understood the concept. "I shouldn't get to play with something I really like for a whole year."

Time was a concept she had a problem with, however. "I think a week will do. What should that favorite thing be?"

She glanced aside, then up at him. "My angel book."

She loved that book, so not having it for a week would be stern punishment. "I think that's fair."

"I must have left it in the angel lady's truck."

"We'll get it tomorrow." She nestled her head against his chest and he rocked her. "I love you with my whole heart."

"I love you with my whole heart, too, Daddy."

He picked up a book and read it to her, then just held her until she fell asleep. Eventually he carried her to her bed and tucked her in, pausing to touch his face to her cheek and smooth her dark hair.

He wouldn't have been able to go on living if anything had happened to his Meredith.

Back in the living room, the woman still slept. Charlie added a log to the fire and sat across from her. She had a few dark streaks on her cheek and in her hairline. He got a wet cloth and dabbed it on her face.

She opened her eyes. That incredible blue gaze wreaked havoc with his senses every time she turned it on him.

"There was still some blood," he explained.

Her eyes drifted shut.

He removed the dried blood gently, smoothing her

hair back from her temple with the cloth. Her hair was so pale and fine; it darkened visibly when it got wet. The skin of her temples seemed almost translucent, and her brows were fair and shaped like wings. Her golden lashes lay against her cheeks in soft curls.

He'd never seen anyone so *exquisite*—there was just no other word for her—*beautiful* didn't cut it, couldn't describe those striking cheekbones and hair that begged to be touched. His fingers itched to learn just how silken and soft it would be.

Charlie wiped his palm against the thigh of his jeans.

In the firelight, her hair shimmered like gossamer threads of silver and gold. He touched it then, just to move it from under her cheek and make her more comfortable. It was cool and satiny in his fingers. He drew a breath that came from his toes and curled a hitch in his chest.

Her eyes opened.

His breathing stopped.

"Charlie," she whispered sleepily.

It was the sexiest word in the history of language. "What?"

"Is it still snowing?"

He roused himself from his visual trance to go peer out the window into the night. The moon revealed swirling flakes still falling to blanket the countryside. "Yes," he answered.

"Charlie," she said again.

If he didn't guard his reactions to every sigh and word and each flutter of her lash, he was going to lose all self-respect. "Yes?"

"Do you suppose I could have a bath?"

Ohmygod.

"I'm kind of achy." She brought her open hand to her chest. "Probably from the seat belt, but I'm thinking a warm soak would feel good."

"You're in luck, then. I just happen to have a whirlpool in my master bath."

"Oh, that would be heaven."

Damn near. "Let me help you. Are you dizzy?"

She sat up and brought a hand to her temple. "A little."

"Wait while I go fill the tub." He hurried to run hot water and turn on the jets, add Meredith's bubble bath, then returned for Starla. He slid one arm around her waist, and she wrapped hers around him and steadied herself. They walked that way, hip to hip to the hallway, and then he guided her ahead of him with both hands on her shoulders.

"Here are towels and a robe." All he had to lend was his own. He helped her sit on the corner of the enormous tub. "Tell you what. You just sleep in my room tonight. While you're in here, I'll change the sheets. Then I'll take the sofa."

"Are you sure?"

"Positive."

Her hair draped over her shoulder in a silken wave. He opened a drawer and pulled out an elastic band. "Here. It's Meredith's."

"Thank you." She smiled up at him. "You're a sweet guy, you know that?"

She captured her hair in a loose knot on her head, then, bending to remove one sock, she swayed.

"Whoa." Charlie caught her by the shoulders and balanced her. "Here." He knelt in front of her. "Bending over probably isn't a good idea." He picked up her foot and peeled the sock away. Her feet had turned him on with socks, he didn't dare look now. He looked straight ahead at the Hawkeyes emblem on his sweatshirt.

She steadied herself with a hand on his shoulder.

After pulling off the other sock, he purposely stared at the mounting bubbles in the tub. "Can you get your jeans?"

She straightened up in her sitting position, reached under the sweatshirt and unbuttoned and unzipped.

It was obvious that she'd have to bend over, so he took control. He could do this. Not everything was about sex. This was about helping a person his daughter had managed to get into this situation. "Stand up."

She did. The sweatshirt hung over her hips, thank God.

Charlie reached under it, concentrating on finding the waistband, located it and jimmied the denim down over her hips, his fingers coming in contact with warm skin and satin in the process. This activity would raise any man's blood pressure, and he'd been without a woman for a long time. She'd said he was sweet. If she only knew. She had to know. "Okay, have a seat again."

She sat. Concentrating on the task alone, he pinched both denim legs at the hem and pulled the jeans down her legs and off. His peripheral vision didn't miss the length of slender bare limbs. The most gorgeous woman he'd ever met was getting naked in his bathroom.

"Holler if you need anything." He backed out of the room and pulled the door shut, then leaned his forehead against the wood for a full minute. When water splashed, he backed away as if the door had jolted him with a high-voltage current. Sheets. He was changing the sheets now. He tucked and smoothed, found an extra clean blanket.

Charlie saw the room as she would view it. A man's room. Practical. Simple. He imagined her pale hair against the plain navy-blue sheets and pillowcases, her ivory skin touching the cotton... He didn't even know her. He'd never seen her before today, but her presence was the most disturbing experience he'd had in...forever.

He was obsessed. Enchanted. Horny, he wanted to rationalize, but that word corrupted the beauty of what he really felt when he was around her. No, she didn't inspire lust. She inspired awe. A purity of admiration he should be laughing at himself for feeling.

"Charlie?"

He would change his name after she'd gone.

Charlie stepped to the door. "Yes?"

"I'm feeling pretty dizzy. From the hot water probably. Would you mind terribly...helping me, I mean?"

He opened the door enough to speak to her. "You want me to come i-in there?" His voice cracked like a seventeen-year-old's.

"I'm afraid I'll fall and bump my head or something. I don't want to be any more trouble."

Forcing one foot in front of the other, he crossed the

room. He was an adult, after all. This was his bathroom, and he could assist a person in need without slobbering all over himself.

Good God in heaven, there was a pale pink bra dangling from the back of the chair he'd placed there for her; her jeans were folded on the seat, his sweatshirt tossed over those and a minuscule scrap of satin that might have been her underwear was on top of the whole pile....

There were bubbles up to her midchest, thank *goodness*, but her pale shoulders were sleekly wet and slender. With her hair gathered on her head, her neck looked slim and vulnerable...like the rest of her.

What exactly did cardiac arrest feel like?

No, his heart was beating because blood throbbed in the most conspicuous place, and he hoped she wouldn't notice. He picked up one of the towels he'd left and managed to look at her.

Her cheeks were bright pink with embarrassment. She hadn't wanted to call on him for help. He was a complete stranger—and a man besides, and she probably felt awkward and vulnerable. Everything slipped into perspective in that second and somehow he was back in control again.

"Can you stand by yourself? I'll face the other way and hand you back the towel. You just hold on to my shoulder or my arm or wherever you need to keep your balance."

He turned around then, and behind him water sloshed. She took the towel, and then her hot moist fingers clamped on to his shoulder in a firm hold. "Okay. I'm going to sit here for a minute and dry off."

She used the chair behind him. Charlie stared straight ahead at the foggy mirror. Here and there a watery streak revealed a glimpse of flesh and white towel. He got light-headed, too.

"I can't tell you how good that felt," she said.

"Yeah?"

"But now I'm so tired again."

"You can go to sleep. The bed's ready."

"That sounds wonderful. I didn't let the water out."

"I'll do it. Do you have the robe on?" *Please God, let her have the robe on.*

"Almost."

He'd left the door open, and the cool air was drying reflective spaces on the mirror. One of them revealed a length of spine and a swell of hip. Charlie honorably looked the other way. Then back.

The robe fluttered the hot air of the room as she pulled it around her. "Okay. I'm ready. Just let me get my clothes."

Charlie turned as she was gathering her clothing, discreetly tucking the bra and panties between layers of denim. He offered his arm and she took it, leaning heavily on him for balance as he led her to his bedroom and the king-size bed with the covers turned back.

Starla placed her things on a chair, sat on the edge of the bed and tugged the band from her hair. The platinum mass fell over the shoulders of the robe. "Thanks," she said.

"You're welcome. I'll clean up in there and leave you to your rest."

After he'd drained the tub and hung the towels, he passed through to find her fast asleep...the robe tossed to the foot of the bed. He'd have to buy a new one because he'd never be able to wear that one without seeing her in it.

After he changed his name, he would buy new sheets, too—and a different bed. He would never be able to fall asleep in this one again. Not after the most beautiful woman in the universe had slept in it...*bare-assed naked.*

Chapter Four

Charlie was horny. All right? No shame in that. He might as well admit it to himself and move on. About two in the morning, he argued that lack of physical release had never been a problem before. At three-eighteen he acknowledged that, okay, Starla, the trucker from heaven, had never been in his bed—or in his *head* before.

It was no wonder that when Meredith made her way to where he finally slept on the sofa, it was already almost eight o'clock.

"Daddy, *SpongeBob* is on and I usually eat breakfast during *Rugrats*."

He opened his eyes and blinked. "Already?"

She nodded. "I'm very, *very* hungry."

Charlie sat up and rubbed his scratchy jaw. "All right. Give me a minute."

His daughter moved up to lean against his knee. "Did the angel sleep in your bed?"

A vision of his robe tossed to the foot of the bed flashed in his mind, and he forgot to argue the angel tag. "Uh-huh."

"And you sleep-ded out here in your sweatpants?"

"Sort of."

"Can we have panacakes?"

"Sure." He got up and made a trip to the bathroom, looked out the front windows at the falling snow still piling up, then started preparations for breakfast.

Coffee was brewing and he had mixed pancake batter from a box when Starla came out of the bedroom and approached the bar dividing the rooms. Meredith turned from where she sat perched on a stool and smiled at their visitor.

Starla had dressed in her jeans and his sweatshirt—he'd have to get rid of it after she was gone, or he'd forever picture her slim shoulders and the fullness of her breasts beneath the worn cotton. Her feet were bare and her hair was pulled into a loose knot with Meredith's band. "Good morning."

"'Morning," Charlie and Meredith chorused.

Her aquamarine gaze dropped to his chest.

He hadn't pulled on his T-shirt. "Did you sleep okay?" he asked.

She averted her attention and took the stool beside Meredith. "I did, but I woke with a headache."

Immediately, he shook out a couple of capsules and placed them on the counter in front of her, then went to grab a T-shirt and pull it on.

Meredith had the refrigerator door open when he returned. She withdrew a colorful pouch and proceeded to strip away the slim straw and pierce the juice box with it. She set the drink before Starla. "You can have one of my Mickey Mouse coolers. It's juice and it tastes like strawberry."

"Why, thank you." Starla picked up the capsules and swallowed them down with a sip through the straw. After tasting the offering, her gaze caught Charlie's. The drinks were incredibly sweet and appealed to kids. He discreetly set a glass of orange juice within her reach.

The area around the stitched cut on her forehead was bruised, and even the skin beneath her eye looked tinged with purple.

At his perusal, she raised fingers to her temple self-consciously. "I look a fright, don't I?"

In his opinion, she could still win the Miss Universe Pageant hands down. He poured batter on the hot griddle. "Does it hurt?"

"It's tender."

Charlie tended his pancakes and flipped them at the appropriate time. He stuck several slices of frozen bacon into the microwave and set plates on the counter. "Garreth—the doc—said it was a clean cut and he made tiny stitches. You shouldn't have a scar."

"Have you heard the weather report?"

For someone who looked the way she did, she seemed unconcerned about the possibility of scarring. Her attention stayed focused on getting her truck on the road. "I just got up a few minutes before you did."

Starla watched him efficiently prepare the meal. He'd only been up a short while. That explained the bare chest she'd admired upon entering the kitchen. She smiled at his time-saving methods and no-frills breakfast. But thinking *bare* reminded her of last night's bathing process and how he'd assisted her to the bathroom and even out of her jeans and later out of the tub.

So far she knew several things about Charlie McGraw: he loved his daughter desperately; he made a good living—this spacious log home was evidence of that—he was adequate in the kitchen; and he was a gentleman.

The night before she'd been too shaken to pay much attention to the way her rescuer looked; she'd been reliant on his strong arms and comforting tones. Today, with her wits about her, she couldn't help noticing more—and appreciating what she noticed.

He was average height, not overly tall, his hands large and long-fingered, and he used them with a graceful ease she admired. His chest and shoulders were broad and layered with lean muscle, as were his arms. Charlie's hair was a dark rich brown and quite obviously tended to wave when it was on the longish side, which it was now.

"You should probably have a Band-Aid over those stitches," he said, moving to find one in a drawer and tear off the wrapper.

Starla sat still as he moved close and gently held her hair away from her forehead to apply the bandage. Her scalp tingled where he touched her. She could feel the warmth of his body and held her breath. She glanced up at him. He met her gaze.

A look passed between them, an inquisitive and silent hello. Her nerve endings were aware of his nearness. She breathed and inhaled the scent of shaving lather and soap and her breasts tingled. Her reaction caught her by surprise and heat spread up her neck and cheeks.

Charlie backed away slowly. He reached over to a small television on the counter and turned on the morning news, deliberately avoiding looking at her. After a few minutes the national news cut away to the weatherman in their neck of the woods.

Snowstorms were still prevailing in the Midwest, and portions of Nebraska and Iowa were under a winter-storm advisory for another twenty-four hours.

"I guess I won't be leaving anytime soon," she said.

"Not with your injuries. The doc said you weren't to drive anyway."

"It could be days before I can get a special rig out to tow my truck. You said it's in a ditch?"

He nodded.

"I'd like to take a look at it, get my things and lock it up."

"You sure you're up to it? I can go get your things for you."

She studied his face, noting his nice cheekbones and wide sensual mouth. "I'm up to it. I just have a headache. Maybe some fresh air will do me good."

"I need my angel book, too," Meredith said. "It's in your truck."

Charlie glanced at Meredith, who quickly said, "I am

giving it to you for a week, Daddy." She then explained to Starla, "I am grounded from my book."

Starla replied simply, "I see."

Charlie nodded, then lifted pancakes from the griddle onto plates. After placing a stack in front of Starla and pushing the butter and syrup toward her, he prepared Meredith's and cut the pancakes into bite-size pieces.

"Thank you."

"You're welcome, princess." He leaned over his daughter and kissed the top of her head, his eyes drifting shut for a moment before he straightened and poured more batter. The sight made Starla's chest ache.

She couldn't imagine the fright he'd suffered the night before, how terrified he must have been and the possibilities that had plagued his mind when he hadn't known the whereabouts of his child. Even though Starla's own father had encouraged her independence, he'd always been extremely protective. No wonder Charlie McGraw looked tired this morning.

"Will Miss Ecklebe worry about me, Daddy?" Meredith asked.

"No, there's no kindergarten at all this week, remember? It's Christmas break."

Meredith nodded. "How many days is it gonna be till Christmas?"

Charlie glanced at the wall calendar near the phone. "Four."

"That's not much, is it?"

His lips flattened in a grim line. "No, it isn't."

"Do you still gots more work to do on your customers' presents?"

"I have a rocker and a cabinet to finish," he replied.

Meredith turned to Starla. "Maybe you can play Barbies with me while my daddy works. He gots to shut the door to the shop so dust and stuff doesn't get in our house. If I go out there, I have to stay in one little spot."

Starla glanced at Charlie.

"She has a designated play area for safety." He carried his stack of pancakes to the counter and sat. "The restriction chafes the princess's inquisitive nature. If I'm running a power tool, I can't hear her questions."

And Starla knew firsthand how numerous those were. "What is it you do, Charlie?"

"I'm a carpenter. Furniture and cabinets mostly. I arrange outside jobs around Meredith's school schedule so she doesn't have to spend too much time at day care."

"I spent a lot of time with my father, too," she said. "My mom died when I was young."

"Her mama's a angel, too, Daddy," Meredith explained with childish wisdom. "Just like her."

"I told you yesterday that I'm not an angel," Starla disagreed.

"It's okay." Meredith popped a bite into her mouth and chewed before saying, "I won't tell nobody."

Starla looked at Charlie and he shrugged.

"After we play Barbies, we can watch *Lilo and Stitch,* okay?"

"What's that?"

"It's my video."

"Meredith, Starla is our guest and needs her rest."

Meredith noted he kindly didn't mention the fact that she was stranded there because of Meredith's prank.

"She's not here to entertain you," he finished.

"I don't mind playing Barbies and watching a movie," Starla said. "I don't think I have much of anything else to do." She turned to Meredith. "If I get tired, I'll just tell you I need a nap, okay?"

"You can both nap this afternoon," Charlie said.

Meredith rolled her eyes. "I'm *five*."

Starla had eaten half of her breakfast, and while Meredith hadn't been looking, she'd enjoyed the orange juice.

"You finished?" Charlie asked.

"Yes, thanks. The pancakes were light and airy, a nice golden brown."

He raised his eyebrows and grinned. "Thank you, Mrs. Butterworth," he quipped, picking up the dishes.

Had she sounded like a commercial? She'd meant it as a compliment.

Meredith helped him place silverware and plates in the dishwasher. It was obvious they'd done the same chore together many times. Watching them in their well-equipped kitchen, Starla was reminded of all the years she'd wished for such a home. A stationary home filled with momentos and memories, a place where life felt safe and solid. She'd spent too many of her formative years on the road. Meredith was a fortunate child.

"Okay, ladies, bundle up and we'll go face the elements. Starla, you didn't have a coat on when I carried you in, so I'll see what I can find."

Minutes later she pulled on a brown leather jacket that had been worn soft. It was too large for her, but so was the sweatshirt she already wore and the gloves he found for her. Charlie tied a pink scarf over the lower half of Meredith's face and around her hood, then tugged a stocking cap on Starla's head, careful of her stitched forehead, following it with a heavy brown scarf around her neck. She was glad she'd worn her practical lined boots.

The three of them ventured out into the knee-high snow, holding hands and making slow progress. The flakes were coming down steadily, but the wind had died down and they could see clearly.

The drifts were too deep for Meredith, so Charlie picked her up and carried her on his shoulders. He moved ahead to break a path for Starla and she followed in his tracks.

"You okay?" Charlie turned and asked at the end of his long driveway.

Starla squinted into the snow-bright daylight. The cold air bit her lungs, and her nose was already numb. "I'm okay."

The Silver Angel was buried over her wheel wells in a ditch. A thick white blanket layered the cab and windshield, but it and the trailer looked okay. Starla walked all the way around, brushing the hitches clear to check them.

Charlie knocked snow from the door and opened it. He lifted Meredith up first, then assisted Starla. Everything inside looked okay, though anything that hadn't been fastened down was on the floor. Charlie handed her the keys. "Will you want to start it and makes sure it runs okay?"

She tucked the keys in her pocket. "The fuel is gelled by now. It'll have to be towed out and warmed up before it'll start."

Grabbing two nylon bags in the sleeper, she stuffed clothing and personal items into them, including her purse, phone and the logs.

"I got my book," Meredith said, clutching it to her chest.

"I'll put it in my bag to keep it dry." Starla tucked the book safely away. Charlie took the bags from her, then assisted her to the ground. He turned back to maneuver Meredith onto his shoulders and Starla locked the doors and stowed the keys in one of the bags.

They followed the path of their own footprints back. While the girls headed inside, Charlie shoveled a path to the stack of firewood beside the garage. After carrying in several loads of wood, he pulled off his coat and hat, and his dark hair was plastered to his forehead.

Both Starla and Meredith had changed into dry clothing and left their boots and coats near the door. "Meredith directed me to the dryer in the mudroom, and I threw our jeans in. I can take yours, too…after you've changed."

The memory of Charlie helping her out of her jeans the night before was one Starla wouldn't soon forget, but she tried to put it into perspective. He capably took care of Meredith, preparing and cutting her food, bathing and dressing her, so helping her could be nothing more than an extension of that helpfulness.

Could be. How self-deluded was that thinking?

His expression had been a little tense during that scene, now that she thought about it. She wasn't naive. Men and women quite naturally had sexual musings about each other, and that had been the perfect time for thoughts like that. For crying out loud, that episode was over and done, but she'd been thinking about Charlie since she'd seen him without his shirt a little while ago!

With everyone in dry clothing and a fire blazing in the enormous stone fireplace, Charlie explained where he'd be. "My shop's right on the other side of the kitchen, there, through that door. If you need anything, just holler. If not, I'll see you about noon for some lunch."

Having collected her thoughts, Starla nodded.

Meredith bounded toward him for a kiss, which he bent to receive and return, and the next minute he was gone.

"I'll get my Barbies," Starla's new playmate said cheerfully.

While Charlie worked in his shop, Starla had a chance to look around. The interior of the McGraw's log home was an open floor plan in finished wood with high-beamed ceilings and a loft area above. Dark rugs in the living room and lushly upholstered leather furniture kept the look masculine, but added warmth and comfort.

The stone fireplace was set at an angle and above it a grainy antique mirror reflected the room. Father and daughter seemed to manage well together here, and to all appearances were happy and well adjusted.

Meredith missed her mother, however, and the fact was obvious from her conversation and the book she continuously talked about. She interrupted Barbie's camping trip twice to tell Starla the story about the angel, and both times she went into great detail about the story.

"I get my book back in a week, and then I can show you the pictures," she said.

Starla's heart ached for the child. There were still times when Starla wished for her mother's comfort and advice, and Meredith was just a small child.

Something about the little girl's shiny dark hair, her wide inquisitive eyes and doubly inquisitive nature invited Starla to feel perfectly natural in taking her onto her lap and occasionally touching her hair. She'd never spent this much time with a child, never held one on her lap or been so amazed and amused by the comments and questions that flowed unceasingly.

"Did you know a camel can walk a million ways without water?" Meredith asked. The muted sounds of power tools and occasional hammering blended into the background.

"I knew they could store water."

"Yeah, and they can get sand in their nose so they have to close their noses."

"I didn't know that."

"Just like on *Crocodile Hunter.* Remember the one about the man trying to get snakes who was pretending that he got hurt from a snake and he drawed a line on his arm?"

Starla was lost as to what one had to do with the other, but in Meredith's mind, the two obviously had a connection. "I missed that one."

"Maybe they can show it again."

"Maybe." Starla glanced out the window at the never-ceasing snow and experienced a niggle of concern. The McGraw's home was pretty isolated, and the storm didn't seem to be letting up.

The door on the far side of the kitchen opened and Charlie appeared, the sleeves of his flannel shirt rolled back over his forearms. He took it off and hung it on a hook, revealing his muscled form in a snug black T-shirt. He washed his hands at the kitchen sink. "Who's hungry?"

Meredith quickly jumped down, scooped Barbie dolls and accessories into her arms and dumped them into the plastic storage container, missing quite a few in her hurried attempt to pick up. "I am!"

Charlie prepared them tuna sandwiches and heated canned soup, and they perched on bar stools at the counter.

"I don't even know if I'll be able to deliver these last two projects before Christmas," he said as they ate. "I've been listening to the radio and there's no telling how long it will be until the roads out here are cleared. Crews are working in town and on the highway, but the snow is coming down as fast as they can remove it."

"You mean we might not have Christmas?" Meredith asked, her eyes filling with tears.

"Of course we'll have Christmas, sweetie," he said, laying down his sandwich and wiping his fingers before he moved over to hug her. "We didn't get our shopping done, did we?"

"I was gonna buy a pretty sweater for my gramma and wrap it up and give it to her myself."

Charlie got a strained look on his face and hugged her tighter. When his copper-brown eyes met Starla's, she thought she saw guilt there.

"We'll have a wonderful Christmas without shopping," he assured Meredith.

She leaned back and looked up at him, her eyes glistening. "How, Daddy?"

He thought a minute. "We'll make our own presents."

"What about a tree? We didn't buy a tree!"

"We can cut down a tree, Meredith."

"Like *Little House on the Prairie*?"

"Exactly."

"Oh, Daddy!" She threw her arms around his waist. But then Meredith drew back and studied Starla, as if just remembering her. "What about you, Starla?"

She'd been wondering that herself. If she couldn't get out of here within the next four days, she would be here for Christmas. Not to mention the load on the truck that wouldn't be delivered and her father's bonus flushed down the tubes. "I don't know," she said finally. "I was counting on being able to deliver my load and be home in time for Christmas."

"Your family will be disappointed," Charlie said.

"I only have my dad. We don't live near each other. He made his own plans for Christmas, and I was going to cook dinner for some friends."

Charlie's eyes moved over her face and hair. "I'm sorry."

She shook her head. "It's not your fault, Charlie, no need for you to be sorry."

Their gazes locked. It was his daughter who had landed Starla in this predicament, and they both knew it. Neither one of them wanted to mention it in front of her; the situation was understood but not discussed.

"You can have Christmas with us," Meredith said, all previous worry vanished. "You can help us cut a tree and put decorations on it."

"Yes," Charlie said. "I have a ham in the freezer."

"That sounds very nice," she replied sincerely.

They finished their meal and Charlie sent Meredith to wash her hands.

Chapter Five

Starla carried dishes to the sink and stood beside him. "Charlie?"

He turned those dark copper eyes on her. He smelled of cedar. "Yeah?"

"Is there any possibility, what with it continuing to storm like this, that the power lines could be affected and we'd be without electricity?"

"It's a definite possibility that the phone lines will go down, but I have my cell phone in case that happens. And you don't have to worry about power. I have two full propane tanks that fuel my shop and the house."

"Okay."

"There's a freezer in the shop full of meat and vegetables and staples. I even keep powdered milk and eggs. The only thing we'll run out of is fresh produce."

Assured, she gave him a nod.

"Feel better now?" he asked, as though understanding her worry.

"Yes. Thanks."

"Make yourself at home here. Snacks, coffee, tea, whatever you'd like. I have satellite TV, it should be working okay. I have a few movies, but I don't know if there's anything you'd like. Mostly action flicks. Your other options are Meredith's cartoons."

"What type of movies do you think I like?" she asked, just to tease him.

He leaned back against the counter and studied her. "Actually, I think you should *be* in the movies."

His comment caught her unprepared. "How so?"

With one hand, he gestured toward her. "Well. You're probably the most beautiful woman I've ever seen."

Starla had been told she was beautiful before, and the compliment always made her uncomfortable. She tended to believe her looks were subjective; some found her striking, others just found her coloring odd. She only knew it didn't much matter what a person looked like on the outside. "Thanks, but you didn't answer my question. What kind of movies do you think I like?"

He crossed his arms over his chest in a relaxed posture. "Hmm. *Shakespeare in Love*?"

She shook her head. "*You* saw that?"

"No, I just figured you had. *Gone with the Wind.*"

"That's everyone's favorite, so it doesn't count."

He pursed his lips as he thought. "*The Sound of Music.*"

"Come on, you're picking classics now."

"Okay." He studied her a moment. "*Sweet Home Alabama.*"

"Didn't like it."

"*My Big Fat Greek Wedding.*"

"Didn't see it."

His eyebrows rose, then lowered as if in challenge. "*The Lord of the Rings.*"

She smiled. "I love all of those. Especially *The Two Towers.*"

"Really?" he asked. "So what *are* your favorites?"

"Anything Tom Clancy or Robert Ludlum wrote and everything with Denzel Washington or Bruce Willis."

"You *like* action movies?"

"Love 'em."

He chuckled. "I guess I'm your man to get snowed in with, then."

Their eyes met and something purely male-female passed between them. An awareness. A fascination. A falling sensation made her stomach dip.

He wasn't much taller than she, and their gazes were nearly level. If one of them took a step forward, their faces would be close enough to…

"Well." Charlie cleared his throat and pushed away from the counter.

Starla turned away, too, raising a hand to her temple. Her head must be a little woozy yet. "Thanks for lunch."

He nodded and went back to his work.

After about an hour Starla grew sleepy, and Meredith seemed ready to nap, as well, so she tucked her in and read her a book about a mouse that wanted a cookie, followed by the same mouse going to school. Meredith had an impressive library of hardbound books and neat shelves filled with educational toys.

Starla finished the stories and laid the books on a white nightstand beside a photograph. The woman in the frame was holding a smiling dark-haired baby, and Starla knew immediately that she was Meredith's mother. Charlie's wife. She was a pretty blue-eyed young woman, so painfully young looking, with a fresh-tanned complexion and dark hair that curled in wisps around her face.

Charlie's wife.

Mixed emotions flooded her at the sight: sorrow that such a lovely, vital person had been taken before her time, empathy for a girl growing up without a mother, irrational jealousy that Charlie loved her.

Starla left Meredith's room and climbed into Charlie's enormous, comfortable bed. His bedroom had a vaulted-beam ceiling, warm wood everywhere and plush masculine furniture. There were no photographs in here, no signs of a woman's touch. She wondered how long his wife had been dead. Years or mere months?

And then she wondered why she cared.

Charlie fixed them steaks and baked potatoes for supper, and afterward Starla phoned her father from the privacy of Charlie's bedroom.

"Starla! Are you doing okay?" he asked.

"I'm fine, Dad. It's still snowing in Iowa. I'm not going to get the load delivered. I'm sorry."

"It's not your fault, honey, don't you worry about it. All that matters is that you're safe and staying warm."

"I'm fine. The McGraws have a log home, and everything is run with propane, so there's no chance of a power loss. There is plenty of food and wood and everything."

"And they are nice people?"

"Incredibly nice. Charlie has been a perfect host. And the little girl—Meredith is her name—kept me entertained all day."

"What about this Charlie's wife?"

"Charlie is widowed, Dad."

"So it's just you and that man?"

"And Meredith, don't forget."

"How old is Charlie McGraw?"

"I'm not sure exactly."

"Thirty? Sixty?"

"Thirty maybe."

Silence.

"He's a carpenter and he works in his shop during the day. How about you, how are you doing? Have the doctors said when you can get the cast off?"

"Probably in a few days. And then I have to do some physical therapy."

"Strengthen the leg and all," she said.

"Yes. But I have to take a couple of classes, too. Is Charlie nice looking?"

"Yes, he's okay. What kind of classes?"

"Oh, it's just a heart health thing, learning how to read food labels and shop."

"Dad. What aren't you telling me?"

"It's nothing. They ran a few tests on me while I was in the hospital, and they advised me to lose a few pounds and watch my diet—don't say you told me so. My cholesterol is a little high."

"Are you sure that's all?"

"That's it, I swear."

"If it was anything more, you wouldn't have encouraged me to stay in Maine and have Christmas with my friends, right?"

"Right. I had something planned myself, Star."

"I suspected that. We've always been together for Christmas in the past. Who is she?"

"She's someone I met at the hospital."

"She's sick?"

"No, she wasn't a patient, she's a volunteer."

"Oh, I see. What's her name?"

"Edith. Do you want to do a background check? She's a widow with a grown daughter who is a state senator."

She was nosing into her father's private business, but she couldn't help her curiosity. Besides, he'd done the same with her. "She sounds really nice. I'm just surprised. You've never…well, *dated* anyone before."

"Hard to imagine the old man dating, is it? *Dating* is probably the wrong word. We're enjoying each other's company."

"Same difference."

"Tell me more about Charlie McGraw. You said he's nice looking?"

"He's nice looking. He has really nice eyes and…" And every time she got within a foot from him, her temperature rose and her heart lost its rhythm.

"Just be careful, Star."

"Dad, he's not going to ravish me. He's a widower and he misses his wife."

A sound brought her around to face the door—the door she hadn't closed. Charlie stood in the opening.

"Widowed doesn't mean dead," her father replied.

"No, of course not," she said distractedly, embarrassment warming her cheeks. Charlie'd heard her last words.

"Call me tomorrow."

"I will, Dad. Bye." She punched the button on her cell phone to turn it off and tossed it onto the bed. "Sorry," she said to Charlie. "You know how it is. He was asking me a million questions."

"No problem. I didn't mean to eavesdrop. I came looking for my glasses and the door was open." He gestured to a table beside an easy chair. "Reading time again."

"More mice with cookies?"

"Oh, no, more advanced reading this time. Carpenter camels."

"I've heard of carpenter ants, but never carpenter camels."

He picked up his glasses and headed for the door. "No comparison. This camel wears a tool belt and everything. You're welcome to listen."

She shrugged and followed. "What else would I do?"

The camel book turned out to be part of a series, and Starla enjoyed the sound of Charlie's voice as he read, using appropriate inflections for each of the characters. He was handsome in his gray metal-framed reading glasses, and Meredith appeared comfortably secure snuggled against his chest.

She pointed to something on a page and then toward the window and asked, "Why is the moon always different? Sometimes it's big and sometimes it's only part."

Charlie launched into an explanation of the solar system geared for a five-year-old's comprehension, to which she replied simply, "Oh."

Continuing, he read three of the stories before telling her it was bedtime. Father and daughter disappeared for about fifteen minutes. Starla flipped through a consumer guide book until Charlie returned. He picked up the books and a pair of small white socks and laid them on the back of a chair. "The child is a nonstop font of questions."

"I'd noticed."

"While she brushed her teeth, I had to explain where the water running out of the faucet comes from," he said.

"Where does it come from?"

He raised a brow.

"No, really, where does it come from?"

"We have a well."

"Oh." She sat forward and placed the book on the coffee table. "You have an incredible home here."

He sat on the chair adjacent to the sofa she occupied. "Thanks."

"Are you content to be so far away from town?" She leaned back comfortably on the sofa. "I mean, is that why you bought out here?"

"I built the house myself. Well, from a kit and with some help. But yes, I wanted the distance." He got up and went to the kitchen, where he ran water. "I'm making coffee. Want a cup?"

"Thanks, but I'd never sleep tonight."

He stood and leaned against the end of the bar while the coffee perked and the aroma teased her senses.

"Speaking of sleeping, Charlie. I feel guilty for taking your bed and making you use the sofa. I'll sleep on it tonight."

"No need." He gestured upward. "There are two more bedrooms in the loft. I just put you in my bed last night because it was close to the tub and you were light-headed. I slept on the couch so I'd hear you or Meredith during the night. You can take your pick of rooms up there and have your privacy. There's a bath with a shower, too."

"Okay. Thanks."

"Don't be thanking me. My daughter is the reason you're stuck here."

"She's a great kid."

"Yeah." He turned back to the kitchen and returned minutes later with his steaming mug of coffee and a cup of herbal tea for her.

She accepted the mug and inhaled the spicy fragrance. "Tea?"

"I keep it for my mom. She's not a coffee drinker."

"You're very thoughtful. Thank you." She blew across the surface and took a sip.

"I have to say you're sure taking this well. I know this is a huge inconvenience. I have a feeling there's more you haven't said."

At his pointed look, she admitted, "Well, there was a bonus connected to this load."

"And now you won't get it?"

"No."

"Is the load perishable?"

She shook her head. "No, thank goodness."

"You don't seem resentful. I guess that's what I find remarkable."

"Wouldn't do me much good to spend a lot of negative energy being resentful," she replied. "No one deliberately set out to sabotage my trip. Meredith is just a child and she had no idea that her actions would cause a problem. The truck ending up in a ditch was an unfortunate accident. I could probably blame myself for that, but I won't."

Charlie just studied her for several moments. She resisted the impulse to self-consciously reach up and touch the Band-Aid or the area beneath her eyes that had bruised. "How long have you lived here—in this house, I mean?"

"Built the house the year before Meredith was born."

"So you and your wife built it together?"

He nodded but didn't embellish. So far he'd never spoken to her of his wife. Meredith was the only one who brought her up.

"Tell me about your town," she said to draw the topic away from her. "What's Elmwood like?"

"Everybody knows everybody. One doctor, post office, a couple of eating places, a school, a pharmacy, a library. A typical little town."

"So you have a lot of friends there."

"I know everyone," he replied.

She understood there was a difference. "The people at the diner seemed very nice."

He nodded. "Shirley Rumford and Harry Ulrich. I owe them a big thanks for their support last night."

"It seems like a great town to live in. After my mom died, my father and I never lived in one place for very long. We usually kept an apartment, but if I wanted to attend the same school all year, I had to stay with my aunt or my dad's stepmother. When I got to be about twelve and the whole popularity peer thing happened, I grew to hate having to choose between school and being with my dad."

"Doesn't sound like a very stable childhood."

"It wasn't all that bad."

"You and your dad are close, though."

"Yes." She sipped her tea. "What about your parents?"

"I never knew who my father was. My real mother worked for Del Phillips. When she died, he took me home to his wife and family. They adopted me and raised me as their own." At her questioning look, he said, "I kept my mother's last name and they didn't mind."

"They sound like terrific people."

"They are."

"You've stayed close?"

He nodded. "They're Meredith's only grandparents."

"What about your wife's parents?"

"They are Kendra's parents," he said, giving her a name for the first time.

Starla worked to absorb that information. "The family who adopted you...was your wife's family?"

Looking away, he nodded.

"So you grew up with her?"

He nodded again.

A love that had grown from his childhood. No wonder it was so painful for him to speak of her.

"What about you?" he asked, reversing the subject. "Ever been married?"

"No."

He studied her.

"What?"

"Just trying to figure it out. You're not exactly..."

"Young?"

"No, God no! I was going to say hard to look at. But I guess you're just selective, eh?"

"Something like that."

An awkward minute passed. "Would you like to watch a movie?" he asked finally.

"Sure."

He got up, opened a built-in cabinet beside the fireplace and rattled off titles.

"That one," she said, stopping him when he got to *The Hunt for Red October.*

He grinned and took out the slim case. "I just happen to have this one on DVD with surround sound."

Starla slipped off her shoes and tucked her feet up under her on the couch. "All we need is popcorn."

"I can take care of that, too."

For the next couple of hours they enjoyed the movie and the popcorn, and then he showed her the extra footage and behind-the-scenes features and how to operate the remote.

"This is great," she said. "Do you even have to go the movies anymore?"

"Rarely. I buy these online and have them delivered to my post office box in town."

She shook her head. "I remember when it was a big deal to go to a movie."

"I remember when my mom used to make popcorn in a big kettle on the stove," he said.

Starla grinned. "My aunt made popcorn balls."

Charlie scooted the bowl aside with his foot and propped both feet on the coffee table. "So you do have some good memories of your childhood?"

She nodded. "I had fun with my cousins when I stayed with them. We used to run through the sprinkler and set up lemonade stands. Sometimes we'd just lay in the grass and stared at the clouds."

"And picked out animal shapes," he guessed.

She looked at him. "Yes."

His eyes were dark with an unspoken sadness. "I want those things for Meredith."

"What makes you think she won't have them?"

"My two adoptive brothers live a few hours away, but she sees her cousins only occasionally. Five boys, by the way. I wanted to live out here to be away from people, but sometimes I wonder if that was such a good choice."

"The town isn't that far," Starla pointed out. "What is it, about eight miles?"

Charlie nodded.

"And she goes to kindergarten. She'll have friends. Looks to me like you've made good choices for her. She's extraordinarily smart and inquisitive. It's plain that she adores you and that the two of you are quite happy together here. I'd have given anything to have had a home like this when I was a kid."

"Yeah?"

"Yeah."

Charlie stood. "I want to throw another coat of tung oil on a piece before I turn in."

He had just closed the subject, and Starla felt as though she'd been prying. She wanted to ask him if she could come along and see his shop, but she sensed his need to be by himself.

"Do you mind if I look through the pantry and cupboards?" She got to her feet, as well. "I'd like to fix breakfast tomorrow if it's okay. In fact, while I'm here I don't mind cooking all the meals. No insult intended, of course."

"I'm not insulted, but I wouldn't want to take advantage of you. You're our guest."

She carried her cup toward the kitchen, set it near the sink and turned to find him behind her carrying his own. "It would just give me something to do and make me feel useful."

He set down his mug and met her eyes. "Okay, then. If you like."

She gave him a warm smile.

His gaze caressed her hair and her features and made her heart flutter. Starla's breath hitched beneath Charlie's warm perusal. He seemed lonely, hungry, enigmatic in those moments before he turned his attention away. "Okay then," he said again and disappeared through the doorway to his shop.

Starla set their cups together in the sink and stared at them, just then noticing that her heart had to catch its natural rhythm.

From Charlie's bedroom she gathered her clothing and toiletries and carried them upstairs. One bedroom was furnished with a twin maple set, like something either Charlie or his wife had brought from their childhood home. The other held a full-size bed with a mahogany sleigh-style headboard and footboard and matching dressers, a comfortable chair and a desk and television. Starla selected that room, stored her few belongings and showered.

She dried her hair, dressed in her white silk nightgown and dressing gown, and stood before the enormous windows to watch flakes of snow swirling in the darkness. She couldn't help imagining what Charlie had been like when his wife was alive, his family had been complete and when he didn't have that lonely, haunted look in his dark eyes.

She ached inside for his loss and obvious grief. And she envied the woman who had inspired such love and adoration. Sometimes she wondered if she was fated to live out her life as a single woman, never knowing the assurance and completeness of a husband to love her, children to nurture and watch grow.

She had made up her mind to accept her life and be fulfilled in whatever the future held. And except for a lonely day or night now and then she'd been secure in her independence and self-sufficiency. Why she felt more vulnerable and isolated than usual while being here with the McGraws she didn't know. But she wasn't going to give in to the emotions and she wasn't going to let her optimism slip.

In a few days the Silver Angel would be pulled out, she'd be on the road, and this experience would be behind her. Until then she would keep in contact with her friend and assistant manager via phone and handle any problems that came up with the final preparations for the Hidden Treasure's grand opening.

She would just enjoy this unexpected vacation and its pleasant diversion and not let herself think too much. Or feel too much—she could feel a lot for the McGraws if she allowed herself. She wouldn't.

Chapter Six

Waking early, Meredith peeked in her daddy's room to find him sleeping in his own bed. The angel lady must be upstairs. She wished she could read her favorite book but she wasn't allowed to have it for one week. One week was a very long time, but her daddy said it was fair for what she'd done and she believed him. He didn't like to punish her.

Silently she tiptoed up the stairs. The door to one bedroom was standing open, but no one was in there. Starla, the angel lady, must be in the other one. She wasn't supposed to open a door without knocking, but the other door was open a little, so it probably didn't count as all the way shut.

Meredith pushed open the door.

The beautiful lady was sleeping in the sleigh bed that

used to be in daddy's room before he got a new bed. The sun that streamed through the part in the curtains touched her hair and made it look like a halo. It was as pretty and shiny as the angel's hair.

Daddy told her Starla wasn't a angel. He just didn't know. Starla said she wasn't a angel, too, but she prob'ly had to keep it a secret in case everybody wanted miracle dust and there wasn't enough.

Starla's shiny white robe was hung on the corner of the headboard, and as Meredith crept closer, she saw the white gown the angel wore to sleep. She didn't know angels slept. Maybe she was dreaming about what she had to do.

Meredith's gaze darted to the tubes and bottles on the counter in the nearby bathroom. Did Starla keep her miracle dust in one of those? Meredith tiptoed into the bathroom and peered at the containers and the open zippered bag. A little tube of something glittery caught her attention.

But she mustn't get into other people's stuff, that was a naughty thing for sure, so she just studied it closely, then backed away.

Starla opened her eyes and sat up as Meredith moved back into the bedroom. "Meredith? Is anything wrong?"

She shook her head. "I didn't touch nothing."

Starla glanced at the clock. "What are you doing up so early?"

"I was done sleeping," she said with a shrug.

The angel lady's shiny hair fell over her shoulders as she stretched and got out of bed. "Are you hungry?"

She nodded.

"Let me dress and I'll come down and start some breakfast, okay?"

"You can cook?"

Starla's smile was so pretty it made Meredith feel warm and happy inside. "I do okay," she replied.

Meredith wanted Starla to smile at Daddy and make him feel warm and happy inside, too. "Are we going to wake up my daddy?"

"We'll let him sleep a little longer. You can help me cook, okay?"

Meredith moved to the door. "Okay!"

Charlie dreamed he was at a party. It was one of those elusive shape-shifting dreams where people morphed into others and it made perfect sense.

Starla was there, dressed in a shimmering white beaded gown with clusters of diamonds at her ears and throat. She was the most beautiful woman in the room and she had eyes and smiles only for him. He felt ten feet tall. An orchestra played "Winter Wonderland" and he held her in his arms and they danced effortlessly, fluidly. As the music was playing, Charlie was kissing her, stroking her velvet skin and lustrous hair and she made sexy little sounds of appreciation and arousal.

The room and the others fell away and he and Starla were inside the sleeper of the Silver Angel, the radio still playing Christmas music. Snow fell outside, but the two of them were wrapped in a heated embrace and he was preparing to slip himself inside her warm moist welcoming heat. He'd never been so turned on or so hard.

Beneath his hands, her body changed, her hair darkened, and Starla was replaced by another woman. A woman he recognized instantly. Charlie now held his dark-haired wife.

Kendra's eyes revealed how stricken she was at his betrayal.

Charlie shot away from her quickly, backed into the cab of the truck and fell instead out the door and into the freezing snow.

He jolted awake.

He had a hard-on the size of Toledo.

His heart was beating as though he'd been running.

Christmas music floated from the other room.

Pushing out of bed, he stumbled into the bathroom, ran water and stared at his blurry eyes in the mirror. What a hell of a dream. He'd known it would be trouble sleeping in that bed after she'd been in it. He shaved, showered, dressed and had his lust under control when he found his daughter and their guest in the kitchen.

Starla was wearing a pair of baby-blue jogging pants with a wide striped waistband that rode low on her hips and a small fitted sweatshirt that exposed an inch of skin at her waist. The inch might as well have been a mile for the direction in which Charlie's thoughts revolved at the sight.

He made an immediate left turn to the cupboard and the coffeepot and busied himself pouring a cup.

"Daddy, look what me an' Starla are doing! We made scones and we're cutting up fruit!"

"Scones? I don't think I've ever had one." He took a seat at the counter.

"Morning, Charlie," Starla said.

Just her voice brought back the dream and the image of pressing her down on the mattress in her sleeper, warm flesh against warm flesh…. He lost his grip on his mug. "Shit."

"Excuse me?"

"Er, sorry. Good morning." He grabbed a paper towel from the counter and wiped his sleeve.

"Give your daddy his plate, sweetie," Starla said to Meredith.

His daughter reached on tiptoe to push a plate of fruit and a wedge-shaped biscuit thing in front of him. "Thanks."

The scones, filled with nuts and dried fruit, were delicious and he ate three. "Where'd you get the recipe?" he asked Starla.

"It's not difficult to remember," she replied. "Basically just flour and soda and fruit."

Starla ate a scone and sipped tea. A brief glance at her lips against the cup and he ticked off something else that would have to be replaced once she'd gone.

Meredith had nibbled on her scone, but instead dug into a bowl of cereal. "Is your work done now, Daddy?" she asked, milk dripping from her chin.

He nodded and wiped her chin with his napkin. "I finished up last night. Now I just sit by and wonder if anyone will have their presents for Christmas."

"It couldn't be helped," Starla said. "You did your part."

"Can we do something together today, then?" Meredith asked.

Charlie studied his daughter's hopeful expression and felt guilt slice through him. "What would you like to do besides work on Grandma's present?"

"Can we go find our Christmas tree?"

Charlie got up to go look out the patio doors at the weather. The sun was shining and the snow seemed to have let up, though the accumulation was deep. "Looks like an okay day. You know we have to walk through the snow? I'll have to get out that old toboggan to carry the tree home."

Meredith squealed, jumped down from the stool and ran to throw her arms around his waist. "Thank you, Daddy! Thank you, thank you. We'll have the very bestest Christmas tree ever!"

"I'll help you dress," he told her. "You don't have any thermals, so you can wear a pair of pajamas under your snowsuit."

"That's funny, Daddy," she said with a giggle. "Wearing my jammies to go outside."

"How about you?" he said to Starla. "Do you have clothes you can layer? I can find you something if not."

"I do happen to own thermals," she said with a smile. "A trucker is always prepared for a winter emergency."

"Good. Meredith, eat your breakfast so we can go get ready."

His daughter was pleased to obey, finishing her cereal before she darted toward her room.

"I'd better go supervise this," he said and headed after her.

Fifteen minutes later, the three of them, bundled in hats and coats and boots, made a stop at the garage for Charlie to locate the toboggan, mix gas and oil to fuel his chainsaw, and acquire a length of rope. Meredith settled herself on the sled and Charlie stowed the chainsaw behind her, then he and Starla trudged through the knee-deep drifts, Meredith riding behind.

They had all worn sunglasses to ward off the glare of the bright light, and Charlie noticed what a disappointment it was not seeing Starla's eyes. Even so, she was unbelievably beautiful, even with her hair hidden under a red-striped stocking cap, a pink flush on her cheeks. He really liked that old leather coat. Shame he'd have to give it away now.

"How much of this land is yours?" she asked.

"Five acres is all."

"All? Sounds like a lot to me."

"I've had a couple of offers to sell a piece here and there, but I like the idea of having no neighbors."

"You don't seem like the hermit type, Charlie."

"I'm not a hermit."

"You just want to avoid people."

"The hassle," he replied. "I avoid the hassle."

"People are a hassle?"

"Some people." They trudged onward and she didn't say anything more. She probably didn't want to pry, but he felt like he needed to give her more of an explanation. He didn't want her having the wrong idea about him. He wasn't antisocial. "Did you ever feel that you just weren't up to others' expectations?" he asked.

She seemed to think a minute. "You mean that I didn't live up to their expectations?"

"No, I mean that you couldn't deal with what they expected of you anymore."

"Well," she replied, "my dad wanted an entirely different life than what I wanted. I just had to live his way until I was old enough to be on my own. Even then, I guess, I was hesitant to break completely away from him, since he's the only family I have."

"Your life doesn't seem all that different now than it was then, though," he said. "Your dad was a trucker and here you are a trucker."

She laughed a little. "I guess that's how it must seem. The rig is my dad's. I was just doing him a favor by running this load. I've been away from the road for a few years."

"Oh." That information caught him by surprise. "So what did you do over that time?"

"Went to school. Settled down in a place of my own."

Now that made more sense. Starla seemed to want roots. "Where is your place?"

"Maine."

A world away from his life. "I've never been there."

"It's incredible. The freshest air. The best seafood."

Her voice held a passion he envied. He hadn't felt passionate about anything for too long and his apathy had begun to concern him.

"There's lot of trees over there, Daddy!" Meredith called from behind.

Charlie focused his attention on the task at hand and surveyed her findings. "We couldn't fit those in the house, goose. We need something a little smaller."

Starla pointed to a stand of younger trees along a frozen stream. "How about one of those?"

"Those are more like it." They changed direction and he called back to his daughter, "Which one do you like?"

Meredith jumped off the toboggan and found a path to walk where wind had blown the snow away and it was only ankle deep. "I like this one!"

"Of course you do," Charlie said with a smile frozen on his face. "It's the biggest one."

"It is the prettiest," Starla added.

Charlie unwrapped the chainsaw from its canvas covering, removed his sunglasses and his coat, and walked toward the spruce his daughter was admiring. "Stand back by Starla," he told her.

Delightedly, she dashed away to stand with Starla, and the two females watched as Charlie donned a pair of protective goggles. He pulled the cord and the saw came to noisy life. Meredith squealed and covered her ears. Charlie found an appropriate angle on the trunk and started a cut.

Several minutes later the blade cut through the last shred of wood and the tree toppled over.

He stopped the saw and his ears rang. The scent of evergreen and fresh wood bit his nostrils. His senses seemed more alive than usual today.

Meredith scampered over and delightedly admired the tree. "It's smells so good!"

"Let's toss all the loose stuff," he said, scraping away dead needles from the lower branches with his gloved hand.

Meredith got more needles stuck in her mittens than she moved to the ground, but she helped and within minutes they had the tree on the toboggan and tied down.

"There's still room for me, Daddy!" Meredith pointed to the front, where only the freshly cut trunk lay on the front curl of the sled.

"Okay, but you hold on," he told her and settled her in place.

Starla reached for the rope and shared the towing with him, which placed them side by side on the walk toward home. He carried his coat over his shoulder.

A hill they'd gone down on the way took a lot longer to climb going back, and when they reached the top, Starla asked, "Can we take a breather?"

"Sure."

They found a fallen tree and perched on the dead trunk.

Meredith got down and made snowballs.

"A cup of hot chocolate will hit the spot when we get back," Charlie commented. He shrugged back into his coat.

Starla nodded.

Meredith was attempting to roll a snowball to get it bigger. "What are you doing?" Starla asked.

"Making a snowman."

Starla got up and added more snow to the original ball. "You need it a little bigger before you can roll it."

The two of them cavorted in the snow, pushing a ball until it was so big they couldn't shove it anymore. Then they began another one.

Charlie joined in, lifting the sculpture's midsection into place when it was ready and helping Starla place the head. Their snowman was so big, Meredith couldn't reach his head.

"He needs eyes and stuff," she said.

They found dead branches for arms, shaped more for a mouth and nose and Charlie took two nickels out of his pocket for eyes.

"He has beady little eyes," Starla observed.

Charlie took her sunglasses from her face and added them to the snowman. "That's because he has to squint."

They all laughed and Starla removed her hat to add it to their creation. She had an incredible smile. In the sunlight her translucent blue eyes took Charlie's breath away.

"We shoulda brought our camera, Daddy, so we couldn't forget our snowman."

"We should have," he agreed distractedly.

Starla's gaze moved over his face and he instinctively knew that she was attracted to him, maybe even feeling the same pull of sexual tension that had his body responding and making him grateful for the disguise of extra clothing.

His dream came to mind, images of kisses and

touches and silky warm skin...lying atop her and preparing to join their bodies.

Her smile had disappeared and her breath came out in clouds of puffy white vapor. "What are you thinking, Charlie?"

"Nothing."

Her gaze focused on his mouth. "That's what I'm thinking, too."

His brain was as numb as his toes because he thought she'd just said something suggestive. There was no way she'd known what he was thinking. And if she had, she'd have slapped him.

"How do you know what I'm thinking?"

She held his gaze a moment longer, then turned to take her hat from the snowman, shake it and pull it on. Retrieving her sunglasses, she wiped them clean with her gloved fingers and slipped them on before saying, "You're still thinking about that hot chocolate, aren't you?"

"Amazing," he said. "Do you read tea leaves, too?"

"And palms," she added.

Meredith was waiting for Charlie to lift her onto the toboggan. After getting her settled, he and Starla each grasped the rope and pulled it forward. She didn't offer more than her profile.

He was convinced they'd just talked sex.

Chapter Seven

Starla hung up all their wet clothing, threw hats and gloves in the dryer and made hot chocolate while Charlie lit a fire in the fireplace, found a stand for the tree and set it up in the living room.

Meredith danced around the room singing "Jingle Bells" and "Up on the 'Houseroof'" with accompaniment of a tambourine.

Carrying a laden tray into the room, Starla placed it on the cocktail table and called for them to come warm up.

The tree wouldn't have fit beneath an ordinary ceiling, but the vaulted expanse allowed the breathtaking spruce a perfect spot. "I've never seen such a big tree inside a home," Starla said. "I saw one like this at a church when I was a kid."

Charlie perched on the sofa and picked up a steaming mug. "Sorry, we didn't have any marshmallows."

"If I'd have had time I could have made some."

"Made marshmallows?"

She nodded.

"How in the world do you make marshmallows and who would want to?"

"It's not that difficult and I've done it a time or two."

He raised an eyebrow and tasted his cocoa. The warmth slid all the way to his toes. He looked at Starla in pleasant surprise.

"I found the rum in a cupboard. Hope you don't mind that I used it."

His gaze must have slipped to Meredith's cup because Starla said quickly, "No, hers is without."

He smiled. "I knew that."

She had made thick chicken salad sandwiches and handed each of them a plate and a napkin. Meredith sat at the cocktail table as though it was a dining table. "This is yummy, Starla. You're a good cooker."

"Thank you." She glanced at the tambourine on the edge of the sofa, then at Charlie. "I brought my CD case along and I have a few Christmas selections. Do you mind if I put one on?"

He chewed appreciatively and swallowed. "The player holds five. You put them in and select Random."

"I think I can figure that out. Where are the tree ornaments stored?"

"There's a storage room at the back of the house.

After we eat, you two can help me find things and bring them in."

"Do we got a angel for the top?" Meredith asked.

"Honey, we have a star, remember?"

"A star is like you, huh, Starla?" the girl said. "Star. Starla."

"Almost the same," she replied.

The sandwich was delicious. "What's in this? It really is good."

"Curry. I rummaged through your spice cabinet. A lot of them are out-of-date, you know. If you buy prepackaged spices, you should make sure you have fresh ones."

He glanced at her. He and Meredith ate pretty simply. Macaroni and cheese and hot dogs didn't call for a whole lot of added flavors. "I'll try to remember that."

She looked at him and glanced away self-consciously then, as though she felt silly for saying anything.

Charlie enjoyed a second mug full of spiked cocoa before Meredith became impatient. He carried the dishes to the kitchen, then gestured for the girls to follow him.

In the spacious storeroom, he moved aside cartons and bins to get to the boxes on the shelves in the back. He handed Meredith a small container and Starla a larger one, then stacked several in the hallway so they could come back for them.

When all the containers were spread out and opened in the living room, Meredith helped Starla select music while Charlie untangled twinkle lights. The lights took longer, so they ended up helping him and then giving advice while he strung them on the tree.

From his position atop the ladder, Charlie paused for a moment and listened to the upbeat version of "Santa Claus Is Coming to Town." "Who is this group?"

Starla opened a box and took out several packages of glass ornaments. Without looking up, she answered, "I forget."

"You didn't forget, who is it?"

She tucked her hair behind her ear. "The Hansons."

"The Hansons? You mean those blond-haired adolescents who had a group for about a month?"

She threw a bow at him. "Don't laugh, this is a good album. I didn't hear you playing any Christmas music."

She had him there. He'd basically ignored Christmas, except for the extra jobs he'd taken on. Any Christmas music in the house would have been Kendra's and he certainly didn't want to listen to it and be reminded of their last years together.

"I like it, Daddy." Meredith was humming and unwrapping ornaments instead of using the tambourine, so that was a plus, he conceded.

Once the lights were strung to his satisfaction, they hung decorations. All of Meredith's offerings were on the lower half in a charming cluster arrangement. Starla discovered a shoebox filled with handcrafted items made of Popsicle sticks, construction paper and cotton balls. "My goodness, where did these lovely creations come from?"

Meredith smiled and lowered her head beside Starla's, one shiny head of hair so dark, the other so light that Charlie stared at the contrast. "I made them!" his daughter told her proudly. She turned to Charlie. "Where's the new ones I made this year?"

"Stuck on the fridge, remember?"

"Oh, yeah." She scampered off to get them.

Starla watched her go before picking up a snapshot of Meredith framed by painted craft sticks. Globs of glitter sparkled on each corner. Meredith looked younger, but her charming dimpled smile was just the same.

Each item in this box had been packed in tissue as carefully as the glass balls had been. She pictured Charlie storing them the year before. As a single father, he bore the heavy responsibility of raising a daughter and seeing to her physical and emotional needs, but it seemed that he managed the task well. He adored her and Meredith obviously felt the same about him. Christmas must be a sad-sweet time for them both without the wife and mother they'd lost.

Starla looked up and found him observing her again. He was a lucky man to have his daughter and this home. But there was a weariness about him, a sadness that seemed to weigh him down. She recalled Meredith's words that first night when Starla had discovered her in her sleeper. *He's sad,* she had said. *That's why you have to help. If you sprinkle some of your miracle dust on him so he can be happy again, I know he'll find me a new mommy.*

Meredith was very perceptive for her tender years. He was sad. But he didn't seem to be in the market for Meredith's new mommy. He was grieving his wife.

Starla understood that well. Her father had mourned her mother for years and years, only recently enjoying the company of another woman. Many times Starla had felt bad in thinking that her father spent more energy grieving his dead wife than he had providing a home environment for his daughter. Charlie obviously knew the importance of security for his child.

He was attracted to Starla, no doubt about it; there was a simmering physical attraction between them. But that's all it was. He wasn't in the market for anything more, and she was wise enough to keep that in perspective.

"You want to hang these on the tree?" she asked.

He took a few steps toward her and accepted the box. "Did you put up a tree at your place?"

She nodded. "Brought one home the first week of December. I love Christmas."

"A real one?"

She nodded.

"Anyone there to water it?"

That was something she hadn't even thought of, now that he mentioned it. She certainly didn't want a fire hazard sitting in her apartment. "Oh, wow. I'd better call my friend Geri to go over and take care of that."

"He has a key?"

"She," Starla corrected, "has a key. Excuse me." She ran upstairs to get her phone and place a quick call to her girlfriend. After visiting for a few minutes, she returned to find Charlie and his daughter hanging the last ornament. The tree twinkled with colorful lights, but the

decorations barely filled the branches. "I think we need to string some popcorn."

"What for?" Meredith asked.

"For a garland. Haven't you ever strung popcorn?"

The little girl shook her head.

"Do you have regular popcorn?" she asked Charlie. "Not the microwave kind, I mean."

"In the freezer. I have several bags I got from one of the nearby farmers."

"Needles and thread?"

"Sure."

"We're set, then." She found a heavy kettle in the kitchen, added oil and popped the corn on the stove.

"I never had that kind of popcorn afore," Meredith said, listening to the popping sounds with awe.

"Believe it or not, this used to be the only kind of popcorn there was," Charlie said.

"Really?"

"Really. Because there were no microwaves yet."

"Where were they all?"

"Not invented."

"Wow. Did they get invented when I was born?"

"Before you were born."

"And we live-ded here in this house, right?"

"Yes, we did."

"Did my mama decorate the tree then?"

Charlie nodded. "Yes."

"Did she make popcorn for the tree?"

He shook his head. "No. Let's carry the bowls into the other room."

In the living room, he tended the fire while Starla threaded needles and showed Meredith the art of stringing the corn. Meredith ate more kernels than she got on the thread and eventually curled up on the sofa and slept.

"We wore her out." Charlie covered her with a fleece blanket and sat beside Starla to help.

"Coming up with a million questions a day is exhausting," she replied with a smile.

He chuckled and she enjoyed the sound, intuitively knowing he didn't do it often. "I was beginning to wonder if you could do that."

He glanced up. "Do what?"

"Laugh. Well, that wasn't exactly a laugh, but a little sound of amusement did slip out."

"Ha-ha. Was that better?"

"It's okay to laugh, Charlie."

"Thank you, Dr. Phil."

She looked down at her task. He had a way of making her feel foolish, but she couldn't seem to hold herself back from talking to him and enjoying his company. She must be some kind of sucker for a handsome face and a sad story, because he possessed both and she found him fascinating.

A couple of minutes passed.

"Hey," he said.

She looked up to find him studying her.

"I'm sorry."

"For what?"

He dropped his thread full of kernels into the bowl

between them and set it on his other side so nothing separated them. "For being a smart-ass when you're being serious."

"We don't know each other very well," she replied, keenly aware of his nearness. "I should keep my comments to myself."

"How boring would that be?"

She shrugged.

"Al' kidding aside," he said. "I need someone to tell me the truth about myself from time to time."

"I wasn't criticizing."

"I didn't take it that way."

She looked into his eyes and admired the color, so dark and yet so vivid and so different from his daughter's. He sat close enough that she could smell wood on his hair and clothing, the spicy scent that always clung to him, and it affected her as it always did. Her breasts tightened and anticipation quivered in her chest. "I'm a little uncomfortable with how close you're sitting."

"Uncomfortable because you don't like it? Or because you do?"

Getting right to it, was he? She could be straightforward and unashamed about her feelings. Her stomach dipped, but she admitted, "Because I do."

"You're outspoken. I like that about you."

"I'm honest with myself and don't try to be something I'm not."

"I don't think you could be," he replied. "It would show in your eyes."

"The windows to my soul?" she said with a smile.

"Something like that."

"What about you?" she asked. "Aren't you honest with yourself?"

"You have to know who you are to not kid yourself," he answered.

"Who are you?"

"Damned if I know."

"Maybe you only have to know what you want."

His gaze moved across her face, touching on her lips and back to her eyes. "Maybe. How are you in that department?"

"I know what I want." She licked her lips and took pleasure in watching his copper gaze smolder. "And I think you do, too."

The corner of his wide mouth raised in a grin. "Your psychic abilities again?"

"Mmm-hmm."

"All right, Madame Starla. Read my mind."

She closed her eyes in pretend thought. Excitement quivered through her. "You want to kiss me."

She heard his quick intake of breath, felt the warmth of his body, smelled the scent of wood and man that heightened her awareness and titillated her senses.

Starla opened her eyes and found his gaze dark, his eyes hooded. His nostrils flared with his breathing.

"How did I do?" she asked barely above a whisper.

"You're good with mind reading. How are your precognitive abilities?"

She hadn't had fun like this or enjoyed another person's company so much for longer than she cared to remember. Charlie was challengingly witty and surprisingly funny. "It's not an exact science, you know, but there's a good chance I can predict something here and there."

"Shoot."

The words formed in her mind. Heat sluiced through her veins and she felt a tremor begin deep inside. "You're going to kiss me."

"There's always the chance that what you're saying put the idea in my head, and I wouldn't have done it otherwise."

"There's also the chance that you'll talk it to death and Meredith will wake up before you've used the opportunity."

He laughed then. A real laugh that melted her bones. He took her shoulder in his strong grasp, turning her toward him. "God, you're fun."

She didn't need much urging. "I was thinking the same about you."

He leaned forward and she slid her arm around his neck to meet his lips.

Chapter Eight

Charlie didn't kiss as though he was out of practice. His lips moved sensually over hers, warm and seductive in their expert pressure, tasting salty from the popcorn. He moved his hand from her shoulder to slide it into her hair and hold her head steady as he angled his mouth for more intimate contact.

He needn't have bothered, she wasn't going anywhere. Her heart lurched and butterflies swooped in her belly; she couldn't get close enough unless she climbed onto his lap, and the thought did cross her sense-crazed mind.

If the fact that he looked good and smelled great was pushing her over the edge, she'd be in total free fall after experiencing the kiss. What was it about him that drew her in and focused all her senses acutely on the exquisite pleasure he created? *Keep your cool, Starla. Don't make a fool of yourself.*

As if *he* was a mind reader, he nibbled her lower lip, and his tongue traced the edge in a searingly erotic exploration.

Starla's heart raced and her pulse roared in her ears. She accepted his deeper penetration, welcomed it, *encouraged* it with a soft groan and by tightening her hold on his neck. Raising her other hand to his shoulder, she grasped the hard, muscled flesh beneath his shirt and held fast.

Charlie released her head to place both hands on her waist and pull her closer, which was difficult from their positions on the sofa.

Starla gave up all pretense of keeping her cool, and with typical spontaneity, gratified her longing for closer contact. Without ending the kiss and while remaining bent over him, she raised up and over to straddle his lap and wrap her arms around his shoulders.

His response was a groan that started in his chest and played against her tongue. He slid his hands beneath her sweater and brushed his palms up her back. His welcome touch on her skin was like kindling tossed on a hungry snapping fire. A slow somersault of passion turned in her abdomen; her nipples tightened with the extreme pleasure of his touch. She wanted to grasp his wrists and bring his hands around to cover her breasts, but this was a *first kiss*, she reminded herself.

A completely, devastatingly, demandingly, *incredible* first kiss. Starla didn't think she'd ever been kissed like this. She could wait until the next decade for him to move his hands and still be in sensory heaven.

When he did move them, it was to grasp her hips and pull her down harder against his erection. At the same time, he broke the contact of their mouths and met her eyes.

"What are we doing?" he rasped on a throaty breath. He glanced aside and Starla followed his quick gaze to the opposite end of the wraparound sofa where Meredith lay sleeping soundly.

Starla turned her attention back to Charlie. Her lips felt deliciously hot and swollen. She wanted to kiss him again more than she wanted to breathe. "Just a kiss," she said softly, straightening her posture by placing one hand on his cotton-clad chest.

"If that was just a kiss, then what's outside is a just a few flurries."

She couldn't resist a smile. The afternoon took on a momentous life-changing quality that she recognized as one of those moments she would remember forever as an event that had changed her life. The music had stopped, so there wasn't even a song to cover the sound of their heightened breathing or the rapid beat of their hearts. Charlie smelled like wood and sunshine, and she tasted him on her lips. His taste was a seduction in itself. She wanted to touch her tongue to his skin; imagining doing it made her hot with desire for him. Beneath her fingers, his heart beat in tandem with hers.

Take it easy, Starla. Don't go glamorizing a moment

of lust into something it's not. I won't. I'm a big girl. But I want more.

"What am I thinking?" Charlie asked on a whisper.

She studied his eyes, his sensual mouth. "That your daughter could wake up any moment?"

"Didn't cross my mind until a moment ago."

"That I can't really read your mind?"

He shook his head.

She dared to hope when she responded, "You're thinking about later?"

"As much as I want that—" his body and his eyes proved that was true "—I really can't handle a complication."

"I'm not complicated," she replied, assuring him that she understood he didn't want more than a temporary distraction. She wasn't one to take sex lightly, but there was something about Charlie and the way he made her feel that she didn't want to let slip by. She was willing to accept a brief relationship on his terms.

Charlie raised his hands to her shoulders and pulled her close to cover her lips with his once more. He slid his fingers across her cheek in a delicate caress, and she imagined them on her breasts, her thighs, her belly, envisioned him touching her, arousing her. An expectant tingle went through her body.

Charlie ended the kiss and said with his mouth against her cheek, "Later, then."

His words promised pleasure. And even though he released her and she moved away, the smoldering desire in his eyes backed up the vow. Somehow they finished the day going through the motions of normal activity. Starla finished the strands of popcorn while Charlie packed the ornament boxes and carried the cartons back to storage.

By then Meredith was awake and she helped Starla hang the homemade garland on the tree. Evening cast its winter darkness and, together with the snow, encased them in the privacy and peace of the warm comfortable log house.

Starla had never enjoyed preparing for Christmas as much as she was enjoying this time with the McGraws. And they weren't even her family, she thought as she realized how remarkably at home she was feeling. She'd happened into the comfort and security of an intimate haven.

Charlie, Meredith, their loving relationship, the house, the snow and the overall mood all played a part in the feelings of cocooned serenity and salvation.

Dangerous maybe. Probably. Undoubtedly. None of this was real. None of it was secure. She was a stranger passing through their lives. She would be gone soon and they would go on as if she'd never been here. But as long as she knew that, as long as she kept it in perspective, why shouldn't she enjoy her time here for what it was?

She intended to. And she intended to make the most of it in the short time she had. Why shouldn't she?

While Starla read a book, Charlie took his daughter into his shop, and they spent a couple of hours working on the gift for his mother. It was a project Charlie had started some time back. The wood needed to be stained and varnished. Meredith loved that part, and he enjoyed their time together. He should have thought of letting her help a long time ago. He'd been preoccupied and he was only just now recognizing what he'd been doing to his relationship with his child.

Later, after they'd eaten, Charlie watched Starla and Meredith load the dishwasher and caught the look Starla cast him beneath her lashes. He didn't know if it had been luck that brought her to the Elmwood diner only two nights ago, or fate that had dropped her off at his door in a blizzard, but he wasn't stupid enough to pass up a good thing when it landed in his lap. Literally.

He handed her a plate and their fingers brushed. It amazed him still that a woman as incredibly beautiful and as charming and as much fun as Starla would even look at him twice, let alone be sincerely lusting for him as badly as he was for her.

Okay, he didn't need a mask to keep from scaring small children away, but he was no Brad Pitt. He wasn't particularly tall—Starla stood nearly eye-to-eye with him, which didn't seem to matter to her. He had nice hair, he guessed and preparing healthy food for Meredith and himself had kept him in relatively good shape. Starla seemed to enjoy his company. Didn't expect anything of him. Made him laugh. Made him hard. Made him crazy.

Charlie felt more at ease around her than he had around anyone he could think of and he barely knew her.

Why was that? He found himself being uncharacteristically playful, saying things he wouldn't normally say, being a person he'd never been with his wife or any other woman.

He felt confident in being whomever he wanted with Starla. She had no preconceived notions about him—he could project anything he wished. She didn't expect anything from him or want anything from him—nothing except his body perhaps, for a brief time. No hardship there.

She was comfortable to talk to, fun to be around, safe to play with. *Because she's leaving.*

He pointedly ignored that thought. "Time for bed, sweetie," he said to Meredith. "Brush your teeth and I'll be right in."

"You'll read me a story?"

"Maybe even two."

Meredith squealed and dashed to her room.

While Starla added detergent and started the wash cycle, Charlie leaned against the counter and thought over their talks. Somewhere in the midst of all that banter about honesty and playful talk about kidding oneself, a lot of truth had been revealed. When Starla had asked who he was and he'd responded damned if he knew, he had been directly on the mark.

Charlie had never had the freedom to learn who he was. He was a responsible son, a dependable husband, doting father. He was everything that others expected of him, but nothing he had deliberately chosen for himself. He hadn't really even picked his own wife.

A knot of remorse formed in his gut at the thought.

When he'd been orphaned at a young age, the Phillips family took him in as their own. Kendra had been gracious and kind, just like her parents, and the two had become friends and childhood sweethearts. When they reached high school age, everyone thought Charlie and Kendra were the perfect couple, and Charlie's adopted parents were no exception.

The blush of young love had faded—for Charlie anyway—but by that time the town had linked their names and expected a wedding. Wed they had, but they'd grown apart and eventually, after Meredith was born, they'd slept in separate rooms. Charlie could never have disappointed the Phillipses by divorcing their daughter.

He was not resentful, never had been; the Phillipses were wonderful people, and he loved them. He'd loved Kendra in his own way. But he hadn't been *in love*. And he bore his share of guilt for that. She'd deserved better than an obligatory husband.

Charlie watched Starla wipe the counters and rinse out the dishcloth. He had never been attracted to his wife in the way he was to this woman. She had loosely fastened her hair up in a clip, revealing her slender neck and delicate ears. Yesterday the thought of kissing that neck would have been a dream, tonight it was an anticipation. His blood ran thick and hot at the promise. She wanted him!

Starla turned out the kitchen light and faced him. "All finished."

A quiver of anticipation zigzagged up his spine.

There had never been anyone before Kendra. And afterward, well, Elmwood was a small town. He'd had a few casual relationships, but as soon as he was seen with someone, the local gossips had them walking down the aisle, so he simply avoided that particular noose and had even considered moving away. But he could never take Meredith from her grandparents. They were her only family. So he stayed. And had very few opportunities for carnal pleasure.

"I'll be back after story time," he said.

She picked up a cup of tea she'd made for herself. "I'll look for a movie. Unless you want to play a game or something."

Always offering him choices, this woman. He smiled. "Okay, a game."

She moved gracefully toward the living room and he went to tuck in Meredith. Of course his daughter chose two long stories that night, and Charlie did his best to do them justice. Meredith had fallen asleep by the end of the second one, so he tucked her in with a lingering kiss on her forehead and turned out the light. He left the room, shutting her door.

Starla had lowered the lights and set up the checkerboard on the heavy coffee table and pulled it nearer the fireplace. "This okay?" she asked, looking up.

The firelight created shadows on her exquisite face. Just looking at her took his breath away. "This is great. I'll get us a drink."

He opened a bottle of wine and returned with it and two glasses to sit at an angle from her where he could lean back against a chair. He poured them each a glass and they tasted the wine.

Starla set her glass down. "Want to make the first move?"

His brain fuzzed over for a moment, but he collected his senses and looked at the game board. "After you."

She turned the board so that she had the black checkers and moved one.

After several moves, she jumped one of his men. Two plays later and she had another. "Are you concentrating?"

He shook his head. "Do you really want to do this?"

Her gaze moved across his face. "I'm not sure what you're asking. Have you changed your mind about…?"

"Lord, no. I'm asking if you want to play this game or if you'd rather just get right to what's on our minds."

She smiled then. "What *is* on our minds, Charlie? I mean, are you thinking about more of what happened this afternoon…you know, seeing how that works for us…or are we thinking about, well, sex?"

He was definitely *thinking* about sex, but he didn't want to rush either of them into anything. "I don't really have a plan," he replied easily. "I'm pretty flexible."

"Can we just see where things go naturally?" she asked. "Without too many expectations?"

"You don't know how perfect that sounds to me," he replied, appreciating her frankness and her reluctance to rush.

She picked up her glass and took a sip.

The next move would be his, and he should put her at ease as she had with him. He reached across the space separating them, took her free hand and urged her closer. She scooted across the floor until they were hip to hip and he could place his arm around her while she shared the chair as a backrest.

They sipped their wine and watched the fire. There was no rush, no expectation, and the silence was comfortable.

"Have you ever been married?" he asked her finally.

"Not even close. You know I was on the road with my dad a lot, and then I went to college, but I was intent on my studies. I hung around with a few guys, but nothing serious."

"But you've been in relationships."

"A couple." She turned and looked up at him. "Are you asking me how many guys I've slept with?"

"No. I'm asking about your life. I'm curious."

She turned her gaze away.

"And initially I guess I was asking to make sure you didn't have a husband."

She sat forward and frowned at him. "Charlie! Do you think if I was married I wouldn't have told you right off?"

"I don't know. You could be estranged."

"And if I was, then what? You'd care?"

"Well, yeah, I'd care."

She snuggled back against his side. "Good."

He lowered his face and smiled against her hair. Inhaled. Closed his eyes to savor the sweet enjoyment of having this woman to hold.

Starla could afford to be selective, and the fact that she seemed even slightly attracted to him blew his mind.

She didn't want him to expect anything of her. Ironic, because he had no idea what to expect. She was mysterious and unpredictable. She was perfect. And she was here for the time being. What more could he want?

A log shifted in the fire, and sparks flew up the chimney. She placed her glass on the table and leaned into him, her warmth and softness traveling like liquid flame up his side and through his blood.

What more could he want?

Chapter Nine

Charlie wanted her, Starla could tell, but he wasn't demanding or hasty. Having lost his wife, he would probably enjoy her companionship as long as things stayed uncomplicated. That was up to her. He had a lot to offer, even without love or commitment, and in order to enjoy it herself, she simply had to let go and flow with the experience.

Charlie. She even liked his name. It was an unpretentious name. Like the man. "Is your name Charles?"

"Yes."

"What's your middle name? No, let me guess." She looked up into his smiling eyes.

He placed his other hand on her shoulder.

"Perhaps your middle name is Shortribs, or Sheepshanks, or Laceleg?"

Charlie laughed, a full-out chortle that came from his toes, and she loved that she could amuse him. "You heard us reading Rumplestiltskin, didn't you?"

She shook her head. "Didn't have to, read it to her myself yesterday."

He finished his wine and set the glass aside. "Well, no, but you're warm."

She leaned toward him and placed a finger on his chin. "David."

"No."

"Richard."

"No."

"William."

He raised his brows. "How'd you do that? You saw something with my name on it."

"I'm psychic, did you forget?"

He reached behind her head and fumbled for the clasp that held her hair and within seconds the barrette was out and her hair draped her shoulders. "Come on, how'd you guess so easily?"

"Simple. Charles is a classic no-nonsense name, so it only figures that your middle name would match."

He ran his hands through her hair, and her scalp tingled. She felt his touch all the way through her body. Her skin responded by warming.

"What's your middle name?" he asked.

"What, you can't guess?"

"Probably not in a million years. If it's logical to assume that the first name matches the middle, which I don't know is a sound theory, by the way, Starla is pretty unusual. But it definitely suits you."

"So you don't want to guess?"

"If I guess it, will you spin straw into gold for me?"

"That's not how the story goes at all, and you know it. If you guess it I spare you some terrible fate."

"The little man in the fairy tale intended to take the queen's child if she couldn't guess his name. You've already returned my daughter. So what will you not take from me?"

"What do you want to keep that I could take away?"

He brought his hand to her jaw and caressed her cheek. "My better judgment?"

As if she could influence him to that degree. He seemed pretty grounded in all areas as far as she could tell. Her heart fluttered all the same. "You'll never guess it anyway, Charlie."

"Then you can have my good sense." He tucked her hair behind one ear and traced the ear with his finger. "Moonbeam."

She grinned. "Nope."

"Luna."

She shook her head.

"Venus."

She pulled a face. "No."

His hands tightened on her shoulders and his expression grew serious. "Angel?"

She shook her head.

"Angelica."

"You're not going to guess it, Charlie."

"I've only just started."

She figured their time could be better spent. "It's Astrid."

He tipped his head. "I might have gotten around to that."

"Not in a million light-years, you wouldn't have."

"You don't know that."

She laid her hand along the side of his jaw, the texture of his skin like an aphrodisiac to her rising greed—she wanted to experience more of him and she didn't want to wait. "But it would have taken you all night and do you really want to guess names all night?"

"I don't care what we do as long as you're right here."

She touched a fingertip to his lower lip, remembering the pleasure of his mouth that afternoon, and leaned closer. "Surely you have some kind of preference."

"It doesn't matter what subject we're on, I always get the feeling we're talking about sex," he said with a seductive tilt to the corner of his mobile lips. He lowered his head until they were mere inches apart. "Not that either of us is expecting anything."

"Exactly." Tilting her head, she met his lips, the sweet taste of wine mingling with the heady flavor of Charlie. She *had* expected something. She'd expected his kiss to unnerve her and create these tingling feelings, and she wasn't disappointed.

They intuitively tilted their heads to a better angle for deepened contact. Starla forgot to breathe.

The first time she'd seen him, that night at the café,

she'd recognized his intensity, and her first impression had been accurate. Charlie was a man of strong passions. She imagined what being with him would be like if he loved her, and that fantasy ignited a new fire in her being.

Holding her head steady with both hands, he pressed damp kisses across her cheekbone, then down her neck in gently nipping bites before leisurely working his way back up to nuzzle her ear. He took his time, breathing her in and making her feel desirable and valued. The feeling was heady without being smothering and she relished it.

Starla had been telling the truth about having had only a couple of relationships. But she'd had numerous dates and met many men who had only one thing in mind—the conquest. Their single-minded selfishness was a turnoff she'd learned to avoid in her teens, and her caution had served her well over the years.

Whatever it was about her appearance that made people think she was aloof and self-assured was a facade. She was as vulnerable and uncertain as the next person, possibly more so, because she couldn't be certain the attention was sincere.

These brief moments had already increased her knowledge about Charlie. He was a rare and gifted spirit, a partner who knew lovemaking was more than joining bodies for physical release. He was a man who knew his strength and prowess and harnessed them for the sheer pleasure of foreplay.

Charlie's lips covered hers again, with mind-drugging pressure—not too hard, not too gently—and she shut out all other thoughts, all memories and disappointments and hopes and simply…felt. Charlie.

Shifting her position so that her legs were to the side, she faced him. When had a kiss ever been such a magic pleasure ride? When had she ever given herself over to the simple enjoyment without demands or unease or second thoughts? When had a kiss ever been a gift rather than a deed?

She pulled back slightly and framed his face between her hands. "Kissing you is like opening a gift, Charlie."

He ran his hands up her back beneath her sweatshirt, clamped them gently over her shoulders and pulled her close to nip her chin. His breath grazed her neck. "A good gift?"

"A lovely gift. Anticipated and unexpected at the same time. Kissing you is like knowing you have a gift in your hands, but having no idea what's inside. At that moment, anything is possible."

"Unless you open it and are disappointed."

"Don't wreck my analogy, Charlie. I was sharing how delicious it is to kiss you."

"I appreciate the encouragement."

She kissed his jaw, the underside of his neck, opened her mouth against his skin and tasted him. He made a sound in his throat that she felt beneath her lips more than heard. His hands on her shoulders lowered to gently caress her spine. At that moment she wanted to reach for his hands and bring them forward to cover her breasts, but she didn't want to be the one to rush. All in good time. Maybe not even "all" right away. They'd agreed to go slowly with no expectations.

So she simply enjoyed the leisurely caresses and covered his lips with hers once more.

His tongue traced her lower lip and she opened her mouth to accept the deepened contact. Their positions immediately seemed unsatisfactory, and Charlie had obviously felt the same because, pausing the kiss, he encouraged her to lie down. Pillowing her head with his palm, he stretched out beside her and picked up the exploration where it had been interrupted.

Nothing with Charlie was awkward. His smiles and touches, his kisses and caresses, were devastatingly honest and unassuming and she was perfectly at ease, just as she'd been in his home and with his company ever since she'd met him. Everything with Charlie was...inflaming...stimulating...provocative.

Charlie came up for air. "Is the floor too uncomfortable?"

Not that she'd noticed. She shook her head.

He kissed her again, a soul-stirring kiss that ignited her senses and spoke to her heart. He moved his weight ever so gently until his body pressed along the side of hers, and his arousal nudged her thigh. Her heart leaped with the thrill of anticipation.

He rubbed her sock-clad foot with his, an intimately sweet caress.

"Charlie?" she said, regretting that she had to separate them to speak to him, but needing to say what had entered her thoughts.

"Hmm?"

"We're not alone in the house, you know. Are you comfortable with where we are and what we're doing?"

"So far. But I take it you're not."

"Not really. I'm not a parent, I'm not used to having a kid in the house."

"Meredith sleeps like a rock, and even if she wandered out here, I don't think seeing us kissing would damage her for life, but I appreciate your discomfort. What would you like to do?"

"Do you want to go upstairs? Oh my, that seemed like an invitation, didn't it? And we're not rushing, so I didn't mean to—"

"Don't overthink it, Starla. You're just saying how you feel and there's nothing wrong with that. I didn't take it any other way." He sat up and pushed to his feet, then reached for her hand. "But I don't want to go upstairs. I'd rather we went to my room if it's all the same to you."

Standing, she was grateful he pulled her close and kept her in his arms. "Sure. I mean, either one is okay with me."

He kissed her leisurely, then extricated himself to bank the fire and turn out the lights. Taking her hand, he led her to his darkened room, where he closed and locked the door. "Lights on or off?"

"On," she replied easily. "I like seeing you."

He hesitated only a moment before turning on a bedside lamp.

She looked him over, from his dark rumpled hair,

down the expanse of his broad sweatshirt-covered chest, across jeans with interesting creases and shadows to his feet in white socks and back up to his half smile. "What's so amusing?"

He shook his head. "You're just so unexpected. A month or…or even a week ago I could never have dreamed up someone like you dropping into my life—" his voice lowered seductively "—or into my bedroom. You're like a Christmas present, too."

"Charlie?"

"When you say my name…well, it has an effect on me."

"I've never talked so much with a man."

"Is that okay?"

"It's great. With you, talk is foreplay."

He stepped forward and took her hands in his, raising them to his lips. "With you, *looking* is foreplay."

"Don't say that."

He kissed each of her fingers, making them tingle. "Me thinking that you're beautiful bothers you?"

She hesitated. "Beauty is relative. And superficial. And sometimes an affliction."

"Then you admit you're beautiful."

"I realize some people think I am."

"And you don't want me to be one of them?"

"I don't want what you think of my looks to be the reason you…want me."

"I understand." Her words made perfect sense. Charlie appreciated her feelings. "I think you're the most incredible looking woman I've ever laid eyes on, but that isn't the only reason I'm attracted to you. Hey, if looks were everything, you wouldn't be here with me now."

She framed his face with both palms. "I happen to like the way you look, too."

He took her hands and placed them around his waist, pulling her close. "You smell incredible. Like citrus shampoo plus something kind of powdery and feminine. I could press my nose against your neck and..." He did so, inhaling and pressing his body to hers. "And wow."

She sighed with what he hoped was pleasure.

"I can't help wondering if you smell this good all over."

She chuckled. "I hope so."

Then, as if his words had assured her, she turned her face to his and kissed him.

"And you're a great kisser," he added against her lips.

"Are you trying to assure me now?"

"Yes."

"Okay, I get it." She released him and crossed her arms over her waist to grab the hem of her sweatshirt and in seconds pulled it off over her head to reveal a deep-rose-colored bra and creamy-looking skin. Her hair settled back across her shoulders, and Charlie's breath hitched in his chest.

He caressed the skin above the fabric, lowered his face and nuzzled between her breasts. She did smell that good all over.

She was incredibly receptive and responsive to his

touches, and encouraged, he reached around to her back and found the hook to unfasten her bra. She helped him slide it down her arms and it fell to the floor while he covered her rounded breasts and tested their weight and incredible softness. Her nipples were hard points against his palms.

Starla's eyes closed and she leaned into him, bringing her hands to the front of his shirt and grasping the fabric.

He pressed another leisurely kiss on her welcoming lips.

When he'd first seen her that evening at the café, he would never have guessed he'd be so fortunate as to have her in his arms like this, half-naked and returning his kisses with fiery enthusiasm. He was so hot and ready for her, he feared he'd burst with the slightest provocation.

"Can I touch you?" she breathed against his lips.

He had his sweatshirt off in record time and, grasping her elbows to keep her with him, backed toward his bed. He fell backward and she landed on top of him, her hair a pale curtain of cool fragrant silk against his cheek and neck.

Straddling him, she flattened her palms and explored his chest with electrifying touches; her caresses extended to his shoulders and neck and down his belly. Charlie closed his eyes and experienced the gratification of her cool hands on his heated skin.

She was incredible to look at and even sweeter to touch. His gaze unerringly fondled her breasts in the lamplight. His jeans and her sweatpants were a sweetly torturous barrier between them.

He raised himself to a sitting position with Starla in his lap so he could reach her breasts. She helped by rising to her knees. With his tongue, he wet the skin, then blew on it. She drew in a breath of surprise. He treated her other breast to the same tactile delight.

Both nipples turned to hard peaks. Starla threaded her fingers into his hair and watched him as he continued the sensual teasing. Finally he took one into his mouth and suckled.

She rubbed her pelvis against his erection in a motion mimicking intercourse and Charlie groaned against her skin.

She pressed him back on the mattress and took a position above him, kissing his chest and licking his nipples in a similar fashion. She brought her mouth up to his and they locked in a deep and impatient kiss.

Pausing the contact long enough to move to his side, she skimmed off her pants and underwear in one sweep. She reached for the button of his jeans, but he brushed her hands aside to hurriedly rid himself of the barrier. Jeans, underwear and socks landed in a pile on the floor.

Chapter Ten

Starla took her time gazing at him from top to bottom, with a lengthy pause in the middle where she studied his erection with an appreciative expression in her clear blue eyes.

"Can I touch you, Charlie?" she asked again.

"You don't have to ask. Just be forewarned that you're playing with dynamite."

"Warning taken."

When she wrapped her fingers around him, he groaned an R-rated curse, but the language didn't inhibit her inciting caresses.

He couldn't imagine anyone or anything feeling as good as Starla and her unrestrained lovemaking. He'd never known a lover to show such genuine delight in giving and experiencing pleasure the way this woman did.

"Charlie," she said, her voice low, but laced with concern.

"What?"

"We didn't talk about something."

"In the bathroom," he said, intuitively. "I'll be right back." He left her with a promising kiss and found condoms in a drawer.

When he returned and tossed them onto the night table, she had stretched out and was waiting with her head propped on one hand. She was the most flawlessly beautiful woman he'd ever laid eyes on. He'd been captivated from the first moment, and now…now that he saw every glorious inch of her, now that he'd been enlightened by the knowledge of her inner beauty, as well, he didn't know how he could be so lucky.

Instead of lying beside her or covering her body with his as was his first instinct, he sat beside her and ran his hands over her skin, from her slender thighs to her delicate feet, up to circle her navel and knead her breasts, then moving on with attention to her shoulders and neck.

"I love the way you smell," she said to him. "That's how I knew we'd be good together."

He touched her lower lip with one finger.

Her tongue darted out to taste it.

He buried his face in her hair, stroked her belly, then the tuft of pale hair below. He used his palm to cup the pad of flesh over her pubic bone and knead it.

Starla closed her eyes and caught her lower lip with

her teeth. Her nipples pebbled in hard points, and he used his other hand to stimulate them.

Charlie slipped a finger into her slick folds and her hips rose to meet his strokes.

She twisted toward the night table and retrieved a condom. In seconds he was sheathed and raised over her, his arms trembling with restraint. "I don't know how long—"

"It doesn't matter," she assured him. "Here, let me…"

He bit back a groan.

"Oh, Charlie."

Just his name from her lips was enough to set him off. He covered her mouth with his so she couldn't say it again and buried himself deep. So deep a shudder ran through his body.

She gripped his shoulders hard and cradled his hips with her knees. Her body arched against his.

"Wait," he said.

"No."

"Starla, hold still…."

"I…I can't." Her breath caught in her throat. She grasped his hips and dug her nails into his flesh. She gripped him so tightly, her strength surprised him.

"Now," she said, "please, now."

She didn't have to say *please.* The word at such a time made him feel humble and powerful all at once. Charlie gave himself over to the pulsation of her sweet body around him, using every last ounce of his strength to encourage her soft cries and rhythmic shudders. His own climax took him by surprise with its intensity.

He lay with his face buried in the soft lee of her neck, her hair cool and fragrant against his face. Beneath him, her muscles relaxed and she loosened her hold to stroke the damp skin of his hip and thigh.

Charlie slid to the side to relieve her of his weight, but lay with his head on her shoulder and caressed her breast. "Sorry it was over so fast."

"Don't." She reached up to cover his lips with her fingers. They tasted salty. "It was perfect."

He moved his head to look up at her. She had been more impatient than he, so he knew her words were sincere.

"We have plenty of time," she said softly. "It's a long night."

He felt himself stir against her thigh, surprising them both, if her raised brows were any indication.

She smiled.

Charlie turned his nose against her skin, inhaling the erotic scents of Starla and sex. He knew what she meant about smelling him and knowing they'd be good together. It was a totally physical and carnal reaction, but absolutely honest. Right now everything about her aroused him, even more so than before he'd known the pleasure of her mouth and hands and body.

He urged her to her side facing away so he could nuzzle her back with his nose and mouth and caress her satiny bottom. Her backside was nicely rounded and curvy and he hadn't paid it nearly enough attention yet. Within minutes he was kissing it, nipping the skin and stroking her thighs.

Starla's knees deserved a thorough exploration, as well as her slender calves and delicate feet. He discovered she was ticklish, and she wouldn't let him touch the soles.

He caressed his way back up her body, indulging himself in the satiny delights and moist crevices, kissing her breasts, her mouth, her collarbone, and enjoying her indulgently passive role this time. Her clear eyes were bright with passion, her lips swollen and parted, and he watched her face as he used his hands to arouse her once again.

The sheets and blankets had been strewn onto the floor long ago, and their activity now had Starla's head on the edge of the bed, her hair cascading off the side. Charlie climbed her body, ran his tongue up her neck and wedged his knee between her thighs.

She wrapped an arm around his neck and pulled him down for an impelling kiss. Taking hold of her, he changed their positions and planted her atop him. She sat astride, this time no clothing impairing the contact, and rubbed against him.

He wouldn't have asked or expected her to take him again, but she initiated the union, raising up to lower herself on his erection. How had this good fortune befallen him? he wondered, his mind in a pleasure-induced fog. Was he going to wake up any moment to find himself dreaming?

Starla leaned forward to kiss him, then sat up to stroke their passions to a higher level. It became an erotic dance of give and take, pause and surge, an act so intensely beautiful Charlie's throat closed with emotion. Suddenly experiencing an irrationally possessive attitude, he was jealous of any other man who had seen her body or shared physical intimacy. At that moment he wished he could have her all to himself forever. It was a dangerous thought, so he closed his eyes and his mind and just felt.

Starla loved looking at Charlie, loved how right and natural being with him felt. Other encounters had made her feel one of two ways—like a tool for pleasure—or like a goddess on a pedestal. With Charlie she didn't feel she was playing either of those roles. His confidence empowered her to be herself. His spontaneity endeared him to her, and his raw sensuality set her on fire.

His wonderful hands, strong and callused, bracketed her hips and assisted her movements. At one touch or word from her, he would delay his own pleasure to accommodate her wishes, but his mounting excitement had already triggered her orgasm and she gave herself over to it.

When she opened her eyes, Charlie was watching her. He raised his upper body to meet her for a leisurely kiss. Then in a swift display of strength, he turned her under him and spent himself in her pliant body.

She lay beneath him, boneless and replete, one hand idly tracing his hip, her eyes closed, her mind and body exhausted. Charlie moved to her side and tucked her against him. In moments she slept.

"Charlie?"

"Mmm-hmm?"

"I checked on Meredith. She's sound asleep."

"Okay."

"I turned out the lights, too."

"Okay."

"Is it all right if I stay here? In your room the rest of the night, I mean?"

"Definitely all right."

"Charlie?"

"What?"

"I love your hands on my skin like that."

"Like this?"

"Yes. And…oh…like that."

"You're so soft all over."

"And you're so…well, not soft all over."

"Lucky you."

"Yeah. Lucky me."

"How long do we have?"

"Until what?"

"Until…morning."

"Hours."

"Good."

"Your beard's scratchy."

"Want me to stop?"

"No. Don't stop."

"Shall I…?"

"Yes-s-s."

"Like that?"

"Mmm. Oh. Oh, Cha-arlie."

Starla woke to the sound of the shower running. She glanced at the clock. Meredith would be up soon.

She grabbed her scattered clothing from the floor, pausing only to slip on her sweatpants and sweatshirt, and carried her underwear in one fist. As she unlocked the door, she glanced back at the rumpled bed, sheets and blankets strewn off the bottom and side and experienced a twinge in her heart.

The rest of the house was silent and she ran to the stairway and escaped upstairs into the bedroom without being discovered by Meredith. She didn't know why it would have been so upsetting, but she'd have been embarrassed to have the child see her in Charlie's room.

Turning on the water in the shower, she set the temperature. After stripping off the clothing, she stepped under the spray and enjoyed the hot water buffeting her hair and body. Shampooing her hair, she thought of Charlie's praise and attention for the scents and textures he appreciated about her. Lathering her skin, she remembered kisses and touches too numerous to count and she took pleasure in how much Charlie enjoyed her, tingled remembering how much she enjoyed him.

Toweling off and drying her hair, she put things into perspective. Extraordinary circumstances had led to an extraordinary encounter, one that wouldn't have happened if things hadn't occurred the way they had.

She was immensely grateful for the way the last few days had unfolded. It was likely she'd never see Charlie again once the weather cleared and her truck was towed. But she would always have these unforgettable memories to treasure.

Downstairs a phone rang. She dressed in a pair of jeans and a long-sleeved shirt and pulled on her socks and boots. Prepared for the day and to face Charlie, she descended the stairs.

Meredith was on the floor in front of the entertainment center watching television. "Morning, Starla!"

"Morning, hon."

Charlie was in the kitchen on the phone and as she approached she heard his side of the conversation. "That'll be great, Janet. What time do you think Russ will get here? Terrific. We'll be waiting. Bye."

Charlie hung up the phone. He looked at Starla, and a warm smile tugged his lips upward. "Good morning."

Her skin warmed at the look and the knowledge that passed between them. "Morning."

"Good night?" he asked.

"Fishing?" she replied.

He nodded.

"I had a great night," she told him truthfully.

A pause stretched between them and if they'd been alone, they would have met in a reassuring embrace. Instead, Charlie said, "That was Janet Carter from town. Her husband has a sleigh and he's coming by to get us."

"Really?"

Meredith must have overheard, because she shot past Starla to look up at her father. "With the horse, Daddy?"

"Yep. Tonight is the Christmas program at church."

Meredith danced around in a circle, her dark hair flying. "'Dashing through the snow,'" she sang, "'in a one-horse open sleigh! On the fields we go…'"

"'Laughing all the way,'" Starla joined in and together they said, "'Ha-ha-ha!'"

Meredith giggled.

"Go get dressed, missy," her dad said.

Meredith flew toward her room. "I'm wearing my red dress. Starla, will you fix my hair?"

"I sure will."

"Yippee!"

"Meredith, dress in your warm pants and boots and we'll pack your dress to change into," her father called, then turned to Starla. "Think she's a little eager to get out of the house?"

"Maybe a little." She helped herself to a cup of coffee. "So tell me about this event at church."

"Well, that's just part of it. Elmwood's Christmas celebration lasts most of a day. There's a chili feed at the Waggin' Tongue and tree decorating at the park. There will be ice skating on the lot beside the library. Robbie Perkins owns that land, and he's made an outdoor rink he floods for the holidays. Then there's the kids' programs and a church service."

"You go to church?"

"Usually. Meredith likes Sunday school." He placed a bowl in the dishwasher and wiped the counter. "The church program is a little dressier, so we'll take extra clothing. Do you have something with you?"

"I have an outfit in the truck."

"I'll go get it for you."

"Will people think it's strange if I come along? To town and church with you, I mean?"

"Garreth already knows. We'll have him look at those stitches, by the way. I talked to Shirley Rumford, the lady at the Waggin' Tongue the night you got here, so she's already aware. And the sheriff knows, so that means Sharon, the dispatcher, knows, so that means that by now a lot of people know."

"What will they think?"

"They'll think your truck landed in a ditch after you returned my daughter to me safely and that you're waiting for it to be towed. Not much to think."

Sipping her coffee, she studied the countertop. "You're right. They'd never suspect that after only two days, you and I would…"

"Get it on?"

She glanced up to find him grinning. "Yeah."

"Neither would I have suspected that, sweetheart."

The casual endearment caught her off guard. "Charlie."

His eyes darkened. "My name is a weapon on your lips. Be careful how you use it. And when."

"Just so I do use it…right?"

He glanced toward the other room, then strode forward and pulled her from the stool into his arms for a delicious kiss. Once he released her, she sat back on the seat and he moved to the other side of the counter, but he leaned toward her. "It's going to be…*difficult* to keep my hands off you the rest of the day."

Chapter Eleven

Taking a horse and sleigh ride was like stepping into a Thomas Kinkade painting. Russel Carter had already picked up an older couple who lived farther from town than Charlie, and together they sat squeezed onto the seats with lap blankets and coats adding to the bulk and the warmth.

"Where did you get a sleigh?" Starla had asked Russel when they were introduced.

"I own a second-hand-furniture store and so I travel to auctions all over the Midwest," he replied. "When I saw this, I couldn't pass it up."

"Exactly how far is it from your place to town?" she asked Charlie.

"Eight miles," he answered.

"Look!" Russel called. "Plows!"

Sure enough, on the other side of a sloping snow-laden field, two trucks with blades were pushing snow from a ribbon stretch of highway.

The other couple cheered.

Charlie smiled and she returned it, but it wasn't heartfelt. Soon the highways would be clear, and the rig would have access to tow her father's truck out. The driver would take her to the nearest garage to warm the truck and the fuel. She'd deliver the load, then head back to her life in Maine. Open her restaurant. Of course, that was the plan. This stop was just a delay. Their lives had only collided for a brief moment, but reality would resume.

She wanted it to.

She turned her attention to the countryside and enjoyed the scenery and the brisk air on her cheeks. This was her first sleigh ride and she meant to make the most of it.

The streets in Elmwood had been plowed, and the main thoroughfare was bustling with activity when Russel dropped them off in an open lot, prepared to head out to gather more country dwellers.

"Daddy, can we skate now?" Meredith asked.

"We'd better take our bags to the church first," he suggested. "We don't want to lug them around all day."

"Okay, and then can we skate?"

"Do your skates fit this year?" he asked.

She nodded. "And besides, Miss Lottie keeps a whole bunch of pairs for the kids and she'll be there to borrow them out."

"Loan them," he corrected, then said to Starla, "Lottie Krenshaw is her day-care provider. Meredith still goes occasionally when I have a job that lasts longer than kindergarten."

They caught a ride in the back of a pickup heading toward church and deposited their bags containing changes of clothing for that night. Then they walked toward the skating rink beside the library. Starla heard the music and saw Christmas lights strung on poles around the perimeter before she saw the ice.

"That'd be Birdy Nichols's contribution," Charlie told her. "She brings a setup for music to local events, picnics, dances in the park, everything. But you'll never hear any current music. She's stuck in the seventies and eighties."

Lionel Richie's voice, singing the words, "Hello, is it me you're looking for?" echoed across the street, verifying Charlie's statement.

"She could have worse taste in music," Starla said.

"Yeah, like the Hansons," he quipped.

Starla would have responded, but a male voice called out at that moment. "Charlie! Wondered if you'd make it in."

A dark-haired man a good six inches taller than Charlie walked forward to greet them.

Charlie shook his hand and introduced Starla. "Starla, this is Nick Sinclair, our former sheriff. Nick this is Starla Richards. She got stranded at my place after an incident with Meredith smuggling herself aboard Starla's rig."

"I heard about that. Nice to meet you." Starla offered her gloved hand, and Nick shook it before turning aside. "You have to meet my wife. She was right here a minute ago. There she is. Ryanne!"

A lovely woman with riotous blond curls escaping a knit hat walked toward them, her coat stretched over a distended belly. "Hi, Charlie."

Charlie made introductions, and Ryanne gave Starla a welcoming smile. "I'm so glad Meredith is here. Jamie's friend Benny is out of town, and Jamie's been missing his playmate." She spoke to Meredith, "Honey, Jamie is over there by the hot-dog stand."

"I see him. Daddy will you help me put my skates on?" Meredith asked.

"Sure. Come on. Let's find a bench."

"What size are you?" Ryanne asked Starla. "I brought my skates to loan, because I'm not skating." She placed a mittened hand over her belly. At Starla's reply, she said to her husband, "Nick would you mind grabbing my skates for Starla? They're on the floor of the truck."

Nick kissed his wife's cheek and went to do her bidding. "I have to find things for him to do," she explained. "He hovers. You'd think I was the first woman to ever have a baby."

"This is your second?" Starla asked.

"My first pregnancy," she replied. "Jamie was born to Nick's first wife. But I don't know how I could love him any more. You have any kids?"

"Oh, no," she said, glancing over to where Charlie

was helping his daughter with her laces. "I've never been married."

"I was a career girl myself at one time," Ryanne said with a smile. "Now I do both. I started an antique shop a while back, so I can set my own hours and work around being a wife and mom."

"It must agree with you. You look happy."

Ryanne smiled. "I am. So, you drive a truck, is that what I heard?"

"Well, I drove my dad's truck as a favor. I got out of trucking a few years back and this was a one-time thing."

"Isn't that just the luck?"

Charlie rejoined them and stood by as they continued their conversation.

"So what do you do now?" Ryanne asked.

"I'm opening a seafood restaurant in Maine."

"Oh, my! Are you the talent or the brains and money behind the operation?"

"Both actually. I have a culinary arts, as well as a business degree."

"You're my kind of girl," Ryanne said.

Nick returned with a pair of white skates with blade covers. "Here you go."

"Thanks." Starla glanced at Charlie. "Got your skates?"

He held them up and they excused themselves to find a bench.

Charlie was staring at her as she sat and removed her boots.

She looked up. "What?"

"You own a restaurant?"

"Uh-huh."

"And have a culinary arts degree?"

"Yes."

"You're what, a gourmet cook?"

She shrugged. "Yeah."

"You might have told me."

"You never asked."

"I fixed you canned soup and grilled cheese and…pancakes from a mix."

"I don't look gift horses in the mouth."

He sat down beside her. "All along you must have been thinking what a schmuck I am."

"I was not. You took me into your home and shared everything you had with me. What more is there?"

"Uh. Class?"

She chuckled. "You've got plenty of class, Charlie."

His eyes darkened. "You did that on purpose," he said referring to her use of his name.

"We're alone."

"With fifty people milling around."

"They didn't hear."

"I'm not worried about what they'll *hear*."

"You mean…when I say your name, there's something to be *seen?*"

He looked aside and tilted his chin just slightly as he made the admission. "Usually."

"Only when *I* say it."

"Thank God."

She laughed. "You're one of a kind…*Charlie*."

"Don't, I warned you."

"Charlie," she said with a seductive rasp.

He flattened his lips into a line. "You are so asking for it."

"For what, Charlie?" She batted her lashes, feigning outrageous innocence, then stood. "Come on, are we going to skate?"

"I'll be there in a minute."

"Okay." She shrugged. "Suit yourself. I'll be on the ice." And with that—and a naughty smile—she left him sitting hunched over on the bench, as though he was casually watching the skaters. Starla waved and skated across the ice.

By the time Meredith got hungry, Charlie was more than ready to go into the diner and warm up. Starla had been welcomed into the community, initiated to the rumor mill, questioned about her background and family, and she'd accepted the attention graciously. At the Waggin' Tongue, there was more than chili on the menu, and she and Charlie chose thick, chunky potato soup and warm crusty bread.

Christmas music played from a pink retro stereo behind the counter. Meredith sat in a booth with them and drew a tree on the frosty window glass.

"I fixed you canned soup," Charlie said again as they ate.

"It hit the spot."

"What kind of soup do you make at your restaurant?"

"Shrimp gumbo, tomato bisque, lentil, black bean to name a few."

He set his spoon aside. "The comments you made about my spices make perfect sense now. Oh, and the morning you said my pancakes were, what was it? Light and airy?"

"A nice golden brown, don't forget," she added.

"They came from a mix, for crying out loud, and I called you Mrs. Butterworth. I was wrong, you're frigging Martha Stewart."

"I'm not."

"Julia Childs, then."

"Gee, thanks."

"You know what I mean."

"Let it go."

"Not until I make you pay for not letting on. And for what you did this afternoon."

"You mean for saying Ch—"

He covered her mouth with his hand, then quickly drew it away and glanced around.

"It's just such a sexy name," she said teasingly.

He had that look in his eyes, the one she recognized as desire.

"Gramma!" Meredith squealed. "Grampa!" She shot down from the bench seat and ran toward a couple who had just entered the diner.

Starla laid down her spoon and dabbed her mouth with her napkin.

"My folks," Charlie said, standing to greet them and invite them to share the booth. He sat beside Starla so his folks could slide in together opposite.

Meredith snuggled on the woman's lap in delight.

"Mom, Dad, this is Starla Richards. Starla, my parents."

"Call us Marian and Del," the woman said congenially. "We're very pleased to meet you. Meredith told me all about you on the phone. She said you were as pretty as an angel."

Starla felt her cheeks warm. "I'm pleased to meet you, too."

"We're very thankful that you brought Meredith back safe and sound," she said. "And so sorry that you had an accident and were injured. Is your head all right?"

Starla's fingertips rose self-consciously to the Band-Aid on her forehead. She still had a bruise under her eye. "It's fine. Just a few stitches."

"Well, I hope it doesn't scar, dear. You're such a lovely girl."

"Thank you, but I'm sure it won't show."

"We were half out of our minds with worry when we got the call about Meredith being missing." She lowered her face and kissed the little girl's head. "It's just too awful to even think of the possibilities."

Her eyes misted with tears, and her husband wrapped an arm around her shoulders. "We lost a daughter, you know. Meredith and Charlie are very precious to us."

"Okay, Mom, this is a Christmas party," Charlie said. "Let's get in the spirit."

"Wait till you see my program, Gramma," Meredith said, sitting up and talking animatedly. "I hold up a *M* and sing and everything."

"We can't wait," Marian said.

Del sat forward and folded his hands on the table. "So how's the soup?"

"It's a carb overload, but it's wonderful," Starla replied.

Shirley Rumford took the McGraws' orders and brought them water and silverware.

Charlie resumed eating. "What spices do you think are in here, Starla?"

"Parsley for certain, coarse ground pepper, paprika and cumin."

"I love cumin," Marian said. "Do you cook, dear?"

"Oh, Starla cooks," Charlie said pointedly. "She's a *gourmet* cook, actually. She's opening her own restaurant in Maine."

"What an accomplishment for one so young," Marian said.

"Meaning, where'd you get the big bucks?" Charlie translated with a wry grin.

"Charles," his adoptive mother scolded.

"I drove truck for several years before going to college," Starla said. "Not much to spend money on when you're living on the road, so I saved. My dad helped with school."

"Well, you should be very proud of yourself. I would love to taste your cooking one of these days."

"Me, too," Charlie said.

"I made you chicken salad," she returned.

"So you did."

Marian glanced from Charlie to Starla with a look of interest.

Starla was grateful to see Shirley bring the McGraws' food.

"Meredith, move over now so Gramma can eat," Charlie said.

Meredith obediently moved to sit beside her grandmother.

Starla was warmed by the reciprocal adoration between Meredith and Charlie's parents. Meredith was a sweet and loving child, and the love and influence of grandparents was a blessing Starla herself had never known. The fact that these were Charlie's adoptive parents, but his late wife's biological parents was uppermost on her mind. She couldn't resist studying them for resemblances to the young woman in the photograph on Meredith's night table. It was difficult to feel out of place around them, because they were so darned nice.

The conversation was pleasant, including talk of stranded motorists and holiday plans gone awry. "It doesn't look as though you'll be able to get back to your family by Christmas," Marian said sympathetically. "It's day after tomorrow."

"My dad and I didn't have plans together this year," she explained. "I was going to cook for friends, and they'll get by without me."

"Well, if your truck hasn't been pulled out and you're still here, we'll be more than happy to have you with us," she said. "The local roads should be clear by tomorrow."

"Thank you," Starla said, taking pleasure in the woman's sincere graciousness. "As long as it's not an inconvenience."

"Certainly not."

"Gramma, can I come home with you?" Meredith asked.

Marian turned her attention. "You know that's up to your dad."

"Can I go home with Gramma, Daddy?" Meredith asked hopefully. "I got a toothbrush there."

Charlie's mother smiled at him, waiting for his reply.

"Sure," he said, avoiding Starla's eyes and the hot rush of anticipation at the thought of having her alone for the night. "I do have those deliveries to make. It looks as though my customers will have their gifts for Christmas. I'll come get you tomorrow when the road to town is open," he said to his daughter. "You have to be back home with me for Christmas Eve."

Meredith giggled with delight and smiled up at her grandmother.

"We can bake cookies," Marian said.

"With sprinkles?"

"How about gingerbread men with sprinkles?"

"Oh, yeah!"

Charlie met Starla's crystal-blue gaze then, and recognized his anticipation of the night ahead was mutual.

They lingered over pie and coffee, and once everyone was sufficiently warm and stuffed, they headed back outside where the light was fading. Voices raised in song floated on the cold air.

"Shall we listen to the carolers for a while?" Charlie pulled up his coat sleeve and glanced at his watch. "We have time before we need to get ready for the program."

Meredith surprised Starla by taking her hand as they walked toward the library. Starla glanced back at Marian and Del who followed, and Marian gave her a friendly smile.

A young woman in a long black coat and red hat met them on the sidewalk.

"Miss Fenton!" Meredith tugged on Starla's hand and pulled her forward. "You gots to meet Miss Fenton."

"Hi, Meredith." The woman's cheeks were pink from the cold.

Charlie and his parents greeted her, too.

"This is our town librarian," Marian said, introducing her. "Clarey, this is Starla Richards.

"Hi," Clarey Fenton said. "I was just coming to hear the singers."

"That's where we're headed," Marian said. "Come join us." Charlie's mom had a way of including everyone and setting people at ease.

At least twenty singers stood on risers, their voices blending as though they had practiced "Silent Night" well.

"They're so good," Starla said.

"Most of them are the church choir members," Charlie offered.

Their director used a pitch pipe to get them on key for the next song, and those standing around joined in the singing of "O Little Town of Bethlehem." When Charlie sang along unselfconsciously in a fluid baritone, Starla found it easy to participate. Meredith held her hand on one side and Charlie stood on her other. Starla experienced something she'd never known before—a feeling of belonging and of being a part of something important.

Her restaurant plans were rewarding and she'd enjoyed the challenge and the work. She was anticipating favorable recognition from patrons and reviewers, but somehow this was different. This was community. Families sharing the holiday with tradition and heartfelt emotion.

The sudden sadness that swept over her seemed out of place at such a time, and she worked to tamp it down. She would only make herself miserable if she let thoughts of isolation take hold.

A week ago she'd been content with her own Christmas plans. Now they seemed empty. Lonely. Superficial.

But she had tonight. And tomorrow.

Chapter Twelve

The carolers finished with “Adeste Fidelis,” and Starla joined the crowd in applauding and calling out Merry Christmas. The carolers broke apart, and Clarey joined a few who were chatting.

“Let’s get to the church,” Charlie said.

Charlie’s parents gave them a ride on their way home to change. Charlie found their bags, and Starla and Meredith joined several other females using classrooms and the rest room as dressing areas.

Once Meredith was ready and her hair brushed and braided, she said, “Is it okay if I go with my friend now? Do you need me to help you?”

“No, sweetie, I don’t need any help. You go ahead and see your friend. Just make sure your dad knows where you are.”

"Okay." Meredith danced away, her red velvet dress swirling around her knees.

Starla washed her face and brushed out her hair, then applied makeup, taking special care to conceal the bruising, then changed into her black pants, short jacket and black pumps. She made it a habit to pack for an unexpected occasion, and this outfit was appropriate for dinner or business, so it was her standby ensemble.

The door to the rest room opened as she was packing her jeans and sweatshirt into her bag and Ryanne entered, dressed in a stylish crème-colored dress and flat shoes. She was a lovely young woman, and pregnancy seemed to agree with her. Her gaze took in Starla's appearance. "Oh, my."

Starla glanced down at her clothing, then in the mirror. "Am I dressed all right?"

"You're dressed perfectly. I'm just—well, you're so *striking*. I feel like the Goodyear blimp next to you."

Starla laughed. "I was thinking how pretty *you* looked."

"Thanks. But right now I have to take care of something for about the hundredth time today." She headed quickly for a stall.

"I'll see you later," Starla called and picked up her things.

She stored them where Charlie had before and made her way along a corridor and into a foyer filled with mingling townspeople. Heads turned immediately.

Charlie had been watching for her, but he wouldn't have needed to. He knew the instant Starla appeared, because a hush fell over the gathering, and attention shifted.

So he wasn't crazy and it wasn't only he who thought she was the most incredible-looking woman who'd ever graced the state of Iowa with her presence. He hurried toward her, knowing she'd feel uncomfortable at the attention.

She wore a black pantsuit that made her look even taller and slimmer than ever. Her skin and hair seemed to glow, and the effect of the makeup she wore made her extraordinary eyes even more striking. He couldn't shake the impression that she looked like a supermodel who'd just stepped off a runway.

As lovely as those eyes were, uncertainty and hesitation filled them when he reached her. He didn't touch her, because he didn't want to cast speculation on the two of them, but he stood close and gestured for her to walk beside him.

"This is Starla Richards," he said to the nearest bystanders. And, one by one, he introduced her to the people of Elmwood, hoping to put her at ease.

Leta Ruby worked at Three B's Bar waiting tables evenings and weekends, but she never missed Sunday service or a social event. She was somewhere in her forties with a teenage son who occasionally accompanied her.

Charlie had introduced her to Starla, and Leta was extolling Charlie's virtues. "This is a good man," she told Starla while patting Charlie's arm, "and believe me I can spot 'em. Some of 'em waste their evenings drinkin' and playin' pool and you gotta wonder what their homelife is like. Well, you can usually figure that. I don't see Charlie here, 'cept at church, and he always has that sweet little girl with him."

Starla smiled and nodded.

"Such a shame, losing Kendra that way," she said. "The whole town was just in shock over her death and we still feel so bad for Charlie." She gave him a sympathetic smile. "Your life has never been the same, has it, sweetie? She was always your special girl."

Charlie didn't have a reply, but his reaction was anger at Leta for expressing words and feelings on his behalf. How the hell did the meddling busybody know how he felt? Typical of the assumptions that ran rampant in this town.

Music began playing in the sanctuary, and the crowd slowly dispersed and took seats. Charlie let Leta's words go. She only meant well, no matter how off the mark her assumptions were. His own guilt and frustration were beneath the anger, and those weren't her fault. Leta assumed the best of him. That was *her* mistake.

He had taken Meredith to her Sunday school room where the teacher was organizing the children, so it was just him and Starla beside his folks in the pew.

He carefully held his expressions in check when he looked at her and had made a point not to touch her in front of people. The last thing he wanted to encourage was a tidal wave of gossip, though just having her at his side was probably enough to have started the floodwaters flowing.

The program began with a prayer and a song, then the robed choir moved in procession down the aisle to the back to give the stage to the children. The students put on their production of the first Christmas and the smaller kids sang. Meredith proudly held up her cardboard *M,* which helped spell Merry Christmas, and Charlie's mom reached over to squeeze his hand.

She had tears on her cheeks, tears of pride in her granddaughter, tears of hurt and loss at not having her daughter there to share. He held her hand and swallowed his own disappointments, reburied feelings of guilt and inadequacy.

After the program, coffee and cookies were served in the fellowship hall. Meredith ran to wrap her arms around his knees. "Did you see me, Daddy?"

"I saw you." She let go and he knelt to wrap her in his arms for a hug. "I love you with my whole heart."

"I love you with my whole heart, too, Daddy."

Charlie kissed her cheek and picked her up.

"Starla, did you see me?" she asked.

"I sure did. You were great. And you knew all the words to the songs, too."

Marian approached them then. "Grandpa is ready to go, sweetie. I have your bag and your coat all ready."

Meredith gave Charlie a quick kiss. "Bye, Daddy. I got to go with Gramma now."

"I'll call you tomorrow," he said, setting her on her feet. "You be a good girl."

Marian took her hand and they headed for the hall leading to the foyer.

"I suppose I should be seeing about our ride," Charlie said. "Russ will have several people to take home and we need to get on the schedule."

Starla nodded. "Go ahead. I'm enjoying the coffee."

A few minutes later he returned to find her chatting with Ryanne and Birdy Nichols. "Russ has the sleigh ready to go. He was just pulling up when I went to look for him. "I'll get your things."

"It was great to meet you," Starla said to the two women and followed him.

This time the other passengers for the sleigh ride were the Spaulding sisters, twins in their thirties who ran the local greenhouse and lived in town. "We just made Russel take us for a ride for the fun of it," Ashton told Charlie.

He introduced Starla to Ashton and Èlyssa.

Moonlight sparkled on the snow, bathing the countryside in an ethereal glow. The bells on the horses' harnesses rang out, and the Spaulding sisters sang "Here Comes Santa Claus" in an off-key duet. Laughing, Starla joined in.

Charlie found himself looking at her more than the scenery. She was the most fascinating and fun woman he'd had the pleasure to know. She had her little insecurities, which he'd picked up on and which he couldn't quite comprehend at first because of her extraordinary looks. However, a measure of understanding had dawned that day. Her beauty was part of her hang-up.

He'd seen the way some of the women looked at her as though she was a threat or a competitor. And he'd definitely noticed the way men looked at her. All of them had shown appreciation, but a couple had worn downright lecherous expressions. What was it she'd said when he'd called her beautiful? *Beauty is relative. And superficial. And sometimes an affliction.* Affliction. At the time, he'd thought it was an odd thing to say, but he understood more clearly now.

Charlie's house came into view, and it wasn't long until Russel reined in the horse in the yard.

"Thanks, Russ," Charlie said. "Thanks to you we didn't miss the celebration."

"Glad to do it," he replied.

The Spaulding sisters waved and everyone called out a Merry Christmas.

They trudged through the snow to the door and once in the house shed their coats and boots. Starla still wore her black pantsuit.

"I'll start a fire," Charlie said.

"Want coffee?" she asked.

"I was thinking about wine. Grab one out of the rack."

She returned with a bottle and two glasses and he noticed her shiver. "Cold?"

She rubbed her arms. "The air went right through my coat on the ride home."

"I have an idea. To warm up."

"What is it?"

"We're alone tonight. We can take the wine in the other room and use the Whirlpool. We can enjoy the fire later."

"Sounds...delicious."

Charlie picked up the wine and glasses and headed toward the hallway. "I'll start the water."

She hurried up the stairs. "I'll be there in a minute."

He had stepped into the full tub and nearly sent the bubbles cascading over the edge when she came in and shut the door behind her. She'd changed into a long silky white dressing gown.

He'd lit an oil lamp for muted light, and the fabric of her gown shone like the pale hair she had gathered on her head. With half a smile, she untied the sash and let her robe fall open. The lamplight emphasized the curves and hollows of her body.

Charlie's mouth went dry.

The white fabric pooled at her feet.

He swallowed. Charlie realized then that he was standing naked with his reaction taking shape and that she was enjoying the scenery as much as he.

"I didn't say a thing that time."

"Yeah, well there's the whole audio-visual thing," he replied. "I'm a well-rounded guy."

"I see that."

He lowered himself into the warm water and reached out a hand.

Starla moved to take it and stepped into the tub, his heart nearly stopping as she stood over him for the moment it took her to bring in her other foot and lower herself into the bubbles.

"Watermelon?" she asked.

It took him a second to figure out she was talking about the scent. "Yeah, sexy, huh?"

"Well, I'll never smell a watermelon quite the same way again."

Her smile was as life-threatening as the sight of her body, as his heart testified. He would never smell a watermelon the same way, either. Nor would he look at his bed or his room or his home or hear his name without remembering her. Before, when he'd thought of changing his name, his thoughts had been self-deprecating, now the same idea seemed like self-preservation.

She still wore the makeup that made her eyes look all the more clear and haunting. It was her eyes and hair that made her so incredibly unique, so otherworldly, and again he absorbed the amazing fact that she desired him. However temporary or superficial her appetite for him, it was his good fortune that she felt it at all.

He still held her hand, so he tugged her forward, leaning to meet her for their first kiss of the evening. It was a tentative meeting of lips that blossomed into the familiar heated yearning and deepened to a clash of tongues. Releasing his hand, she moved forward to slide onto his lap, skin gliding against skin in the silken caress of warm water. He pulled her toward him so her breasts brushed his chest and his erection quite naturally rubbed her in what must have been all the right places, because she caught her breath and moved on him deliberately.

"You feel so good," he said, releasing her mouth to hold her close and whisper against her ear.

"I want you now, Charlie," she said breathlessly.

He glanced at the packets he'd left on the tile ledge.

It took a minute to sheath himself and settle back down in the water, but they picked up where they'd left off and she sank down onto him, her body trembling.

"Are you cold?" he asked, though she couldn't possibly be. The water was warm and the jets swirled it around their bodies.

She shook her head and gripped his shoulders. "No, I...I...o-oh, Charlie."

Her internal muscles quaked with her abrupt climax, and Charlie held her hips to guide her movements while kissing her neck and shoulder, gradually building his own pleasure. She took control then, kissing him and moving so deliberately that his own release came in a convulsive crest of sensory indulgence.

He slid his hands up her back and held her tightly. For several minutes he remained with his face buried in the crook of her neck, enjoying every last sensation and feeling the beat of her heart against his. Finally, he leaned back and raised a hand to lazily draw circles of bubbles on her shoulder and upper chest.

She laid her wet palm along his cheek and gazed into his eyes before tenderly kissing him. "I don't know what it is about you, Charlie."

"I don't, either...but I'm grateful for it."

She gave him a tender smile and drew a wet line over his lips with her finger, then kissed them.

"We forgot the wine," Charlie said against her mouth.

She smiled and moved to settle back comfortably in the water beside him.

With suds dripping from his wrist, he reached for the two glasses he'd poured and left forgotten.

"I'll bet we're the only people who attended the program tonight who are now drinking wine in a Whirlpool tub," she said with a sexy grin.

"You might be right," he agreed. "My folks have Meredith, so they wouldn't be."

She smiled. "How about Ryanne and Nick? They seemed pretty stuck on each other."

"Definitely. And they could have sent Jamie home with a friend or relative."

Her brow furrowed. "Can pregnant women have sex in a Whirlpool?"

"I wouldn't know."

"You never…with your wife?"

"No."

Starla sipped her wine. "Does it hurt that much to talk about her?" she asked.

He studied the dew of perspiration on her face and sleek shoulders and thought about her question. "Not really."

"But you don't. Talk about her, I mean. And you're uncomfortable when others do."

"That's a better word," he agreed. "Uncomfortable."

She let the subject drop.

Charlie refilled their glasses.

"You have the perfect home here. It's like a secluded getaway. As you intended, I'm sure. And on a night like this…" She smiled. "The weather outside is frightful and all that."

Charlie raised his hand and drizzled suds across her bare shoulder. "You'd like it here the other seasons, too. There's all kinds of wildlife and a creek that runs across the land to the west. Spring is alive with so many shades of green that you can't count 'em. I've been planting perennials every year and I have a garden with fresh vegetables. In the summer, there's a bank of clover as pretty as anything you've ever seen, and from down by the creek, you can hear the frogs clacking at night…."

Charlie paused, thinking about what he was saying. He'd been rattling on, describing things he loved about his place—things she probably didn't care about—things she wouldn't see.

"Clacking?" she questioned.

He felt numb inside. "It's not a croak really. More of a clacking sound when there are so many."

She wouldn't hear them. She wouldn't be here.

In another day or so, Starla would be gone.

Chapter Thirteen

Wrapped in her robe and nestled in a fleece throw, Starla relaxed on the plump pillows and thick comforter Charlie had arranged before the fireplace. At the moment she was content to lie there forever.

"Are you hungry?" Dressed only in a worn pair of jeans, he hunkered in front of the fire, using the brass poker to arrange a log he'd added.

She turned an appreciative gaze on him, admiring the sleek-muscled breadth of his shoulders and the play of firelight on his corded arms. "Will you cook for me if I am?"

After reaching to put the tool away, he brushed his palms together and sat. "I was thinking along the lines of cheese and fruit. No cooking required."

"Sounds great."

He draped his wrists over his knees. "Want to come along tomorrow when I go into town and deliver the orders? I figured we could pick up a few groceries."

"Sure. Will you be going to your folks for Christmas dinner since the roads will be cleared?"

"No reason not to."

Of course there wasn't. Charlie and his daughter would want to be with their family. Starla couldn't help a little disappointment that the original plan to bake a ham for the three of them wouldn't be necessary.

"Mom invited you."

She nodded. "She's a great lady."

"Yeah. No complaints about my folks." He rubbed her feet through the blanket. "Warm enough?"

She nodded.

He looked as though he wanted to say more. Instead, he leaned toward her, kissed her and stood, heading for the kitchen. Warm and content, she closed her eyes and tucked away memories.

"Want to watch anything?" he called a few minutes later. "Or listen to music?"

Enjoying the crackling sound and heat of the fire, she'd dozed for a moment. "I don't think so. I don't mind if you do, though."

She heard him approach and set something on the floor. Opening her eyes, she discovered a tray of cubed cheese and apple slices. A few crackers lined a plate.

Rolling to a sitting position, she reached for a square of cheese. Charlie stacked food on a small plate and handed it to her. She thanked him and leaned back against an overstuffed chair.

He bit into an apple slice and chewed thoughtfully. "So, how did you get interested in cooking school?"

"I don't know. When I was a kid, I enjoyed time in the kitchen with my aunt. It was a treat to have all the ingredients on hand to bake and create recipes. I was used to eating on the road and occasionally being in an apartment long enough to buy groceries to last a day or two.

"It probably had a lot to do with..." She paused after taking a bite of apple. "With the permanence of a kitchen and pantry and a freezer. Those things were luxuries, and even as a teen I felt secure when I was cooking." She raised a questioning brow. "Think that's weird?"

"No, no, not at all. I get what you're saying."

"Who knows what draws us to the things we like to do? Like you and your carpentry. Was that a childhood dream?"

"Not as exciting as aspiring to be a policeman or a fireman or an astronaut, was it?" He grinned. "In high school, I took to woodshop like a fish to water. It's creative and solitary, two things I liked."

"So your class yearbook says Most Likely To Build A House under your picture?"

"Something like that."

"Can I see it?"

"What, my yearbook?"

"Yeah. Unless you don't want me to."

"Well, no, I don't care. I just have to remember

where it is." Pushing to his feet, he opened one of the cabinets built into the wall beside the fireplace, revealing books and picture albums. He found what he wanted and after glancing at the cover, handed it to Starla.

She rolled onto her stomach and opened the book.

"McGraw," she said, flipping to the index pages and running a finger down the names. Charles was listed on half a dozen pages, and she started with the first one.

It was the football team, and a young Charlie posed with one knee on the ground, his helmet under his arm, in a row of other players. His face was slimmer, his hair longer, and he wore a serious expression.

On the next page she located Charlie wearing a tux and standing beside the dark-haired girl who would become his wife, the same person in the photo on Meredith's dresser. She wore a floor-length dress with slender straps over her shoulders and they posed on the dance floor with a dozen balloons overhead.

"Partners Kendra Phillips and Charlie McGraw, Elmwood High's inseparable duo, are in step as usual," the caption read.

Kendra wore her hair in an upswept style and a radiant smile lit her features. Charlie's hand was touching her waist. Starla forced her gaze away and quickly located the next picture of him in the rows of seniors' head shots. Charlie's good-natured smile was in place on a much younger version of the same man. Beneath his likeness, she read, "Honor roll, student council, varsity football, Y-club." Scrawled around and under were dozens of signatures, "Stay cool" and "You're the man" written in youthful script.

A fascinating peek into his past. There was a lot about Charlie McGraw that she didn't know.

Starla flipped through the pages, glancing at autographs that read, "You and Kendra are a cool couple" and "Kendra is lucky to have you."

His high school sweetheart.

Starla closed the book. He'd said it was uncomfortable to talk about his wife, and it was really none of Starla's business, so she kept her thoughts and questions to herself. She wanted to ask when he'd first known he loved Kendra and about the things they'd done together as young lovers. Some perverse side of her wondered if they'd made love in his car or at a motel—or at all.

Somehow she pictured them crazy in love and sneaking away at every opportunity to be alone. Starla hadn't stayed at one school long enough to have a real boyfriend, and her first sexual experience had been in college. "Honor roll, huh?"

"You're dying to ask me something," he said.

She shook her head.

"Yeah, you are, go ahead."

It probably wasn't cool in a casual relationship such as this to wonder about the other person's past partners. Charlie certainly hadn't questioned her. "It's none of my business, Charlie."

He picked up the wineglass he'd refilled and drank. "You're wondering about my wife."

"I'm curious."

"Everyone said we were perfect for each other."

"You made an attractive couple."

"My mom used to talk about us getting married before either of us had ever mentioned it. She'd say teasing things like, 'If you had changed your name to Phillips, then Kendra wouldn't even have to change her name when you got married.' And we'd chuckle over it. Our names were always linked.

"And when we got to high school, because we lived in the same house, we of course walked together and went home together, and everyone saw us as a couple. At home we were able to talk about things. She was a good sounding board. A good friend."

Charlie fell silent. When he glanced at Starla, she gave him a tender smile. He moved the food tray aside and leaned toward her for a kiss. On his lips she tasted salt from the crackers and the sweetness of the wine.

His mouth moved down her chin and neck and he nudged aside her robe to press kisses against her chest and then her breasts.

Starla moved to lie on the covers and grasp his shoulders, threading the fingers of one hand into his hair. With slow deliberation, he aroused her once again, brought a flush to her skin and made her heart race. This time their joining was leisurely, the kisses sweet and the touches gentle. Their initial passion had been sated and this time was sheer indulgence.

Charlie took his time, building her enjoyment to a crescendo that encompassed her entire body and being, and then following with his own deliberate release.

They lay in the glow of the fire and the aftermath of their lovemaking and dozed, then woke again to share kisses and touches before sleeping soundly.

When Starla awoke next, morning light filtered through the blinds. The delicious aroma of coffee stirred her senses and she pushed up onto one elbow.

Charlie had obviously showered and dressed and now carried two mugs toward her. "Morning, sleepyhead."

"What time is it?"

"Early yet. Barely seven."

Holding the blanket to her breasts, she accepted a cup, and he sat on the floor with her.

She felt self-conscious with her hair ruffled, and quite likely there were sleep creases on her cheek. Charlie's eyes showed only appreciation, however, as his gaze moved over her. He sipped from his mug and Starla did the same, the rich flavor of the brew awakening her taste buds and warming her. "Mmm, this is good."

He nodded, but he set aside his coffee and moved beside her. He slid her hand away so that her breast was exposed and ran his fingers over the swell. "I can't seem to get enough of you."

She would be leaving. Her heart dipped as though she'd plummeted in an elevator. Did he share the same bereft loss she felt at the thought? The same urgency to cram as many memories as possible into the short time they had left? Of course not. She was a winter diversion and he was a healthy male with a heady sexual appetite. She hadn't had enough of him, either, but not for the same reasons.

"I should shower," she said.

"Not on my account." He leaned to close his mouth over her nipple, and the sensation was hot and erotic.

Without further conversation or preliminaries, he removed his clothing, sheathed himself and stretched out over her. The union was swift and purposeful, almost desperate in its focus.

Afterward, he touched her face, kissed her shoulder, and moved to sit beside her.

She rolled on her side toward him and stroked his firm hair-roughened thigh, loving the solid feel of him beneath her hands.

"Starla," he said.

"Hmm?"

"Did your dad have expectations for you? I mean, what did he want you to do with your life?"

She studied his earnest face for a moment. "He taught me his business. We ran together for a couple of years after I graduated high school. I wasn't happy, and he knew it. He knew I wanted roots. When I told him I wanted to go to college, he gave me his blessing and a bank account."

"How did you tell him?"

"I just laid it out as plainly as I could. I'd found all the information on the colleges I wanted to try for and showed it to him."

"He wasn't disappointed?"

"He was happy for me. He didn't really know what

to do with a daughter on the road all those years. He did his best. We were a team. But he was okay with me taking a new direction."

"But you're close now?"

"As close as we can be when he's never in one place. Why do you ask? Are you thinking about Meredith? You have an entirely different situation. She's secure and confident in the home you've provided for her."

He nodded.

She found her robe in the pile of covers and pulled it on, then stood. "I'm going to shower."

Charlie got up and pulled on his briefs and jeans. "The roads are clear. I'm going to load the Jeep. Want to find some breakfast here or eat in town?"

"Whatever you'd like. I'll call and arrange for the tow."

He nodded and tugged on his sweatshirt.

Sitting in the Waggin' Tongue, Charlie remembered the first time he'd seen Starla. It had only been four days ago, but everything had changed in that short time. It felt as if his whole life had been altered.

Starla's cell phone rang. She answered and gave the caller directions to Charlie's road. "Okay, that's great. Thank you."

She switched off the phone. "Day after tomorrow."

This was Christmas Eve. The day after Christmas she'd be gone. An empty feeling yawned in Charlie's gut and he fought back an adolescent urge to hit something.

"I feel responsible for the bonus you lost," he said, his throat thick with the things he couldn't say.

"You're not."

"But I want to repay you somehow. I could make up the difference in what you lost."

"Don't insult me, Charlie," she said, her tone the most severe he'd ever heard.

"But my daughter is the one who—"

"Unforeseen circumstances," she interrupted. "If I'd had you come to meet me instead of driving back here, maybe I would have missed the worst of the storm and you'd have been the one stuck somewhere for a few days. Who knows? It just happened, and my dad understands. There'll be another bonus. Trust me, he's not hard up." She glanced over the menu. "Why have truck stops never heard of fruit?"

"There's a strawberry waffle."

"And the strawberry glaze comes from a can."

"There's orange juice."

"I'll have juice and toast."

When Shirley sauntered over she asked, "Where's Meredith?"

"Spent the night with my folks," Charlie replied.

The woman didn't say anything, but Charlie knew where her thoughts traveled. And her assumptions were on the money.

Starla ate her toast and drank a cup of coffee that didn't taste nearly as good as the cup she'd shared with Charlie that morning.

They ate and Charlie paid, and then he delivered his

projects. Starla got to see a beautifully constructed rocking chair, a small chest with drawers and decorative legs, and a wall shelf. Each piece was uniquely crafted, the wood smooth and finished with detailed carved designs. Charlie was a craftsman, but an artist, as well.

His customers paid him and called holiday greetings. He drove to a grocery store and they shopped, Charlie buying fruit and vegetables and asking Starla to pick up ingredients to cook a meal that evening. She did so and they paid and loaded the groceries.

He drove to a brick home in a lovely neighborhood and parked in the driveway beside a basketball hoop.

Disappointment dampened her spirits. Their brief interlude was over. The end was almost here.

"Is this where you grew up?" she asked, working to sound more cheerful than she felt.

He nodded and took her hand as she got out of the vehicle.

Charlie opened the door without knocking and ushered Starla inside the house. Marian Phillips was a collector. Every wall and each surface was covered with a collection of something, from teddy bear figurines to miniature Victorian houses. She had several pieces of furniture that bore Charlie's signature carvings.

"Hello!" Charlie called.

"Out here," was the reply.

He took her coat and hung it beside his in a closet, then led Starla through a doorway into an enormous kitchen. The walls were covered with spatterware pots and utensils, and braided rugs covered the floor. It was a warm and inviting room with a round table and cushioned chairs, a china cabinet and even an old wooden high chair holding a doll.

Meredith jumped up from the table where she'd been coloring with marking pens and ran to hug her father.

Marian was stirring something aromatic on the stove. "You're just in time for lunch. Starla, I hope you like minestrone."

"I adore minestrone."

Meredith released her dad and immediately hugged Starla around the hips. "I missed you, too!"

"Well, thanks, sweetie." Starla touched Meredith's hair with affection. The child's spontaneous gesture touched her deeply. Children were a new experience for Starla, and she had grown fond of this special one in the short time she'd known her. She swallowed an unexpected lump in her throat and blinked away the threat of tears.

Marian ushered them onto chairs at the table and pushed an intercom button. "Del, it's lunchtime. We have guests."

"Be right there."

"He's putting together another model airplane," she said. "As though there aren't enough in his den. Ah, well, it keeps him busy."

Meredith climbed onto her dad's lap and batted those big blue eyes up at him. "It's Christmas Eve, isn't it?"

"Yes."

"It's a special night tonight."

Charlie nodded.

"Daddy, can I be ungrounded from my book just for tonight? Will you read it to me for a Christmas story?"

Silence hung in the room and Starla's and Marian's attention focused on Charlie.

He'd taken the book away as punishment. No doubt he was torn, wanting to let Meredith enjoy her book on this special night and yet knowing he needed to be firm in teaching her the consequences of her actions.

"Meredith, what you did was wrong," he said. "You could have been badly hurt. You didn't know Starla was a nice lady who would bring you home."

She nodded vigorously. "Uh-huh. I knew she was a angel lady, and angels are good."

"She was a stranger to you," he insisted.

The child's expression clouded and a tear rolled down her cheek.

Charlie resolutely stood his ground. "Starla was hurt because she brought you back. She lost…some of her paycheck because her load is late. All of that is very serious."

Starla felt like the bad guy now, though she knew Charlie was right and that children learn by the results of their behavior. She probably wouldn't make a very good parent, because she'd have given in immediately.

"I'm sorry, Daddy. I won't never do it again."

"I forgive you, Meredith," he said. "You're just a little girl who can't imagine the bad things that could happen. But I have told you many times that you have to ask permission and that you must stay away from people you don't know. Those are the reasons for your punishment."

Meredith didn't cry or display a temper. She simply leaned trustingly against Charlie's chest, her hair touching his chin, and splayed her hand on the front of his shirt.

Starla's heart tugged with empathy for the child and admiration for the man. She glanced at Marian and read similar feelings in the expression on her face. The woman quickly brushed at her cheek and resumed stirring the soup on the stove.

Charlie met Starla's gaze then, and it was plain in his eyes how difficult it was for him to disappoint his daughter in any way. But he obviously loved her so much that he knew the rules were imperative. The glimpse into a very personal part of their lives reinforced feelings of admiration and affection that had taken root in her heart when she hadn't been looking. At the same time, she felt even more like an intruder.

Chapter Fourteen

Starla got another glimpse into Charlie's life when his father showed up at the table. He was a delightful gentleman, and Starla recognized qualities in both of the Phillipses that had led them to take in a child and raise him as their own. They quite obviously loved him as their son. And Meredith held the unique position of being the offspring of both their beloved children, biological and adopted.

Marian's soup was delicious, and Starla told her so. "You used cumin," Starla said with an appreciative smile.

"Don't you love it?" Marian replied. "It's such a robust seasoning."

Charlie rolled his eyes.

Starla laughed. "Marian, you speak my language!"

Charlie chuckled and caught Meredith's spoon before it fell off the table, placing it back in her bowl as though it was second nature to run interference at the dinner table.

"Wait til you see our gingerbread man cookies," Meredith said. "I got some to bring home, and Gramma gots some to save for tomorrow."

"There's enough for each of us to each have one for dessert, too," Marian said.

Meredith clapped her hands and Charlie caught her glass of milk before it tipped over and placed it farther back on the table.

Meredith chattered about their baking and playtime, and Starla recognized the importance of the older woman in Meredith's life. She had missed special times with her mother, but remembered her aunt fondly for those reasons. Every girl needed a maternal influence.

The soup was so good that Starla ate a second bowl before accepting a cookie from Meredith. Marian poured her a glass of milk.

"Oh, my goodness," Starla said in appreciation. "This one has silver buttons."

"You can eat 'em!" Meredith said. "They're candy!"

"This is the best gingerbread man I've ever seen."

Charlie bit the leg off his and walked the cookie around as though it had a limp.

Meredith giggled and bit the leg from her cookie to mimic her father.

Marian placed a tray laden with fudge, divinity and chocolate-covered pretzels on the table. Wide-eyed,

Meredith immediately leaned forward, and Charlie halted her with, "One of each, and that's it."

Eventually Starla helped Marian with the dishes, enjoying the chore because of the woman's pleasant company. Del returned to his model planes, and before long Charlie bundled up Meredith to leave. "We'll see you tomorrow, Mom."

Marian kissed his cheek, hugged Meredith and gave Starla a warm hug, as well. "I can't wait to see you again tomorrow. You'll get to meet Charlie's brothers and their families. They'll be here late tonight."

Starla was touched by her sincere invitation. "I bought a few things at the store. May I bring a dish?"

"Certainly," Marian replied.

Settled in the Cherokee on the way home, Starla said, "So I get to meet the brothers."

"Both of them."

"Older or younger?"

"Older. They were in junior high when the Phillipses took me in. I think I was in fourth grade."

"You said you never knew your dad, but you remember your mother?"

He nodded. "I was lonely and miserable for some time after she was killed and after the Phillipses took me in. But they treated me so well and were so understanding that it was hard not to love them and feel loved in return. I owe them my whole childhood and upbringing. I never had to go to a foster home. It could have been a lot worse, but they gave me a home and a family."

"It's an incredible story," she agreed. "They are terrific people."

Charlie had experienced extreme loss. He'd lost his mother at a young age and his wife in the prime of her life. No wonder it made him uncomfortable to talk about his losses.

"Daddy, we have to wrap Gramma's present," Meredith called from the back seat.

"Yes, we do, but we have to put the hinges on first."

"Did we make something for Grampa, too?"

"We made him the shelf for his airplanes, remember?"

"Oh, yeah, he will like that."

When they arrived at the house, Charlie pulled into the garage and they carried in groceries.

He and Meredith headed for his shop and Starla began the meal. While the dough was rising for rolls, she cleaned all the vegetables and stored them in plastic bags for later use. Then she prepared a seasoned brine and poured it over a rib roast in a bag, sealed it and stored it in the refrigerator to fix and take for Christmas dinner.

Later, when Charlie and Meredith came in to wash, he said, "Something smells wonderful." He glanced in the pot of boiling water. "That can't be what I think it is."

"Why not?"

"Because spaghetti isn't gourmet cuisine."

"Preparing food is an art," she said with a smile. "Even the most simple fare can be elegant when approached with skill."

"So it is spaghetti?"

"Actually, it's linguine. Roasted vegetables and rolls to go with it."

He raised a brow. "And our little grocery had the things you needed?"

She gave him a sideways glance. "I improvised on a couple of the ingredients."

She looked at him, saw the amusement and appreciation in his eyes and wanted to move into his arms…or simply touch him…but they both remained standing where they were. Meredith had gathered her crayons and a tablet and was seated on a stool at the nearby counter.

They enjoyed the meal together, and later Charlie took over dish duty while Starla and Meredith played Chutes and Ladders. Starla worked to simply enjoy the time together, deliberately avoiding thoughts of how temporary this domestic scene would be.

Charlie's thoughts focused on the coming days. Life would not be the same after Starla had swept through and left her mark in a hundred ways.

Evening fell over the log home, and he lit a fire, reminding him painfully of the night before and his time alone with Starla.

"Daddy, let's remember the angel story, okay? Without the book and the pictures."

"Okay," he agreed, grateful for the distraction.

Meredith went through the story by memory, describing the pictures and the characters with vivid recall. He added a line here and there, having read the book aloud so many times. It had been an obsession with Meredith for the past several weeks, and as he heard her tell it in her own words, he heard the story from her perspective for the first time.

He could now see that Meredith missed having a mother. Charlie spent a lot of time in his shop—avoiding life, but all the same, avoiding her. She saw the angel and the miracle dust as a magic solution to having a family come together happily. He couldn't give her back her mother. But he could give her himself.

"Meredith, does this story remind you of us?"

"I don't know."

"I think it does. I've spent too much time working and not enough time being your dad. I'm sorry about that. From now on, we're going to spend more time together. You're more important than anything else."

"I don't want you to be sad anymore, Daddy. I want you to find us a new mommy."

His chest ached with the pain of her childish logic and the impossibility of explaining it on a level she could understand. "It just doesn't work that way, sweetie."

"I like Starla a lot, and she cooks real good. She could stay with us if you asked her. Couldn't she?"

Charlie couldn't look up. He felt as though he'd lost his balance on a sheet of ice. In a split second he was going to fall and break something, and he scrambled to stay upright. Meredith was freely voicing feelings and wishes as only a child could. He didn't want to burst her childish bubble of hope, but he didn't want her getting her hopes too high, either.

"I like Starla a lot, too. But she has her own life far away from here. She has a new restaurant and people working for her and friends who miss her."

"I will miss her, too," Meredith said.

Charlie let himself glance up then, but Starla wasn't meeting his eyes. She was probably embarrassed by the wild assumption on Meredith's part. "I know," was all he could say.

Any more words regarding Starla's leaving would be hollow, so he kept silent. And dreaded the moment when it would happen.

Meredith knew her daddy didn't believe in angels, that's why he couldn't believe in Starla's powers. Meredith hadn't exactly seen the miracle dust, 'cept for that little tube of stuff in her bag on the bathroom counter, but this week she'd seen her daddy smile and laugh a lot more. Since Starla had been with them, he didn't seem as sad as before. He came out of his shop and played games and listened to music. They'd worked on Gramma's and Grampa's presents together and they'd cut down their tree and decorated it.

Daddy said Starla wasn't a angel. Starla said she wasn't a angel, too. Gramma didn't say she wasn't, and Grampa just smiled when she asked him. Starla did seem too real to be a angel, even if she was as pretty as one. She ate and slept and she didn't fly or nothing—at least not when they were looking—but she could fly up to heaven at night when everybody was asleep, though.

Magic things had been happening. Daddy just didn't believe. When Daddy tucked her into bed, Meredith squeezed her eyes closed tightly...and believed.

Late that night, after Meredith was sound asleep, Charlie went to the storage room and gathered the gifts he had wisely ordered online well in advance of Christmas and set them around the tree.

He was surprised to see Starla carrying a small package from upstairs.

"I found it at the grocery store," she said with a shrug. "It's a Barbie she doesn't have." She set it with the other gifts.

Among all her good qualities, he could add kind-heartedness and generosity. Starla was thoughtful of Meredith's feelings and had befriended her from the moment she'd met her.

Charlie took one of her hands in his and kissed her fingers. He feathered the hair from the side of her face and laid his hand along her jaw, just looking at her. With his thumb, he gently touched the darkened bruise under her eye, which hadn't diminished her beauty.

He loved her smile, the way her eyes twinkled when she was amused. He appreciated her sincerity and her tender heart. He'd opened up and talked to her more than he'd ever talked to anyone. Maybe that was because she listened with her whole heart, sometimes not saying anything, but always interested, always understanding.

Maybe he'd talked a lot because he'd been mostly

alone with a child for the past few years and it was a treat to have an adult companion.

Maybe it was simply because she was safe. The thought infused him with a dose of guilt. She'd be gone soon and he wouldn't have to deal with an uncomfortable entanglement. Had he done this on purpose? Deliberately taken advantage of the situation? Christmas could be a lonely time for single people. Keeping things in perspective, it was natural for them to be drawn to each other.

The closer the time came for her to leave, the more pressure built in his chest and the harder it became to remember this was a casual affair. He'd always wavered between thinking there was something wrong with him—some flaw in his character that he'd never felt passionately toward a woman—and wondering if all men felt that way but were better at making others believe they experienced love.

Now he was frightened to think maybe there wasn't anything wrong with him after all, but that he'd simply never met a woman who made him feel strongly.

He led Starla into his bedroom, undressed her in the pale light coming through the skylight and knelt in front of her, pressing his face to her satin skin and holding her close.

She locked her fingers in his hair, and her body trembled.

He made love to her with urgent desperation, using his hands and lips and body to convey the things he could never express in words. He woke during the night to find her gone, the other side of his bed empty and the door slightly ajar. One more night. One more night and even the brief pleasure he'd known tonight would be a memory.

Charlie stared at the stars in the wintry sky and pressed every souvenir into his aching heart.

Chapter Fifteen

Starla woke early and placed her roast in the oven. After showering, she dressed in the black pantsuit she'd worn for the Christmas program, anchored her hair on her head and wore her all-purpose gold earrings and bracelet. She regretted not having more of her wardrobe here to select from, but Charlie's parents didn't seem the type to judge on appearance, and hopefully his brothers were the same.

Glancing at the clock and knowing her dad was an early riser, she picked up her phone and called. "Hey, Dad."

"Merry Christmas, Star. Are you doing okay?"

"Just great. Merry Christmas to you." After telling him about the activities in town and about Meredith's program, she filled him in on the latest preparations at the Hidden Treasure.

"So, you've been keeping in touch with Geri, but I'll bet you're chomping at the bit to get back and get your hands dirty in that kitchen."

She stood looking out the window at the acres of sparkling snow. "It'll be good to get back. I'm invited to the Phillipses' for the day, but I had to talk to you before things got underway."

"Love you, Star."

"Love you, too, Dad. Tell Edith Merry Christmas for me."

"I will. Call when you get out of Iowa tomorrow."

Starla turned off her phone and returned to the kitchen. She prepared a quick breakfast of muffins and fruit and had them waiting when Meredith appeared from the hallway, her eyes alight with excitement. "Santa came! Look, Starla, Santa came! Where's Daddy?"

"He must be asleep," she replied. "Go wake him."

He hadn't been asleep, because when Meredith returned with Charlie in tow, he was dressed in slacks and a sweater and his hair was wet from the shower. "What smells so good?"

"My mustard-glazed pork roast," she replied, "and breakfast."

Meredith tugged him toward the Christmas tree. "Can I open 'em now?"

"Go for it," he replied.

Starla took him a cup of coffee.

Charlie looked her over appreciatively. "You're beautiful this morning."

"Thank you."

Their eyes met and the idyllic night before was revealed in his warm gaze. Not having the freedom to move into his arms was a restriction that saddened her.

Paper ripped and Meredith squealed.

Starla turned and Charlie joined her to watch Meredith open packages.

A mound of paper, books, skates and toys later, Charlie pointed and said, "That one's from Starla."

Meredith picked up the gaily wrapped box. "You got me a present, Starla? Thank you!"

She peeled back the paper to reveal a Barbie. Looking up with wide blue eyes, she said with all seriousness, "I wanted this my whole life."

Touched by her childish sincerity, Starla grinned and helped her open the box. After Starla unfastened the doll from all its packing restraints, Meredith took it and hugged her around the neck. She placed a damp kiss on Starla's cheek.

Starla held her warm, sturdy body close and discovered a feeling she'd never known. The little girl was unrestrained in her affections, honest and open, her innocence a sweet unaffected quality.

With a lump in her throat, Starla experienced a glimpse of the responsibility Charlie bore. Raising and protecting the child was a weighty obligation, one Charlie took seriously. She admired him all the more for his bravery in taking on such a huge life task.

Meredith pulled back. "We have a present for you, too."

"You do?"

"Uh-huh." She turned and crawled under the low tree branches. "Is it here, Daddy? Here it is." She showed the package to her dad first. "Is this the right one?"

He nodded and she handed it to Starla.

When had they had time to buy her a gift? The wrapped rectangle was heavy. She placed it in her lap and tore away the red paper. Inside was a wooden box. The top was carved with a star design, and the wood had been painstakingly stained and polished. She recognized Charlie's detailed carving, and her heart fluttered with surprise. She caressed the finish reverently, thinking of Charlie's gifted hands working the wood.

"Open it," Meredith prompted.

Starla raised the lid. The interior was lined with purple velvet, and a pink plastic ring lay on the fabric.

"I helped Daddy made the box, but the ring is only from me," she said proudly.

Starla took out the plastic ring and slipped it on her little finger. "I love pink."

She glanced at Charlie, who was watching with obvious self-consciousness. "It's lovely, Charlie," she said, her voice not as strong as she'd have liked. "I truly love it. Thank you."

He nodded.

"My gift for you isn't nearly as thoughtful."

"You didn't have to give me anything," he said.

She handed him a small package she'd placed under the tree that morning. He opened it to discover the corkscrew and set of wine markers she'd found at the grocery store.

"I didn't have much time to shop," she said.

"They're great, thanks."

"When did you have time to make this?" she asked, still touching the wooden chest.

"We worked on it when we made the gifts for my folks. Meredith, you did a good job of keeping our secret."

"I never told," she said with a broad smile.

An ache welled in Starla's throat and jaw and she suppressed the sudden urge to cry. He must have spent a few hours during the night a time or two, as well, in order to create the intricate design and sand the wood to such perfect smoothness. Projects like this weren't done as quickly as he let on.

In a way she wished he'd never made it, never given it to her, because it would forever be a permanent reminder of what she'd had to leave behind. And she would keep it forever, she knew.

On the other hand, she was grateful for a tangible reminder of their time together, no matter how painful. She would treasure the handmade gift and be comforted by thoughts of Charlie and Meredith making it just for her.

Starla received another hug from Meredith. Over the girl's shoulder, she looked at Charlie. He got up and picked up wrapping paper and bows.

"I made muffins," Starla said, standing then, and moving toward the kitchen. "And sliced fruit."

If things were different, if they didn't have to hold

themselves in check around Meredith, she would have moved into his arms and thanked him properly. Instead, their exchange seemed incomplete, as if resolution was dangling out of reach.

Starla forced herself to put aside the thought and make preparations for the day.

Charlie's brothers were nothing at all like Charlie in looks, of course, being slender with reddish brown hair and receding hairlines. But along with their wives and children they were a friendly, jovial bunch, and Starla recognized similarities in their senses of humor and interaction with one another that linked them as a family.

Jacob, the oldest brother, was a computer programmer in Des Moines. His wife, Donna, was short and plumpish, with an infectious giggle, and they had two boys, Randy fourteen and Craig, twelve.

Sean and his wife Robyn had three boys. The oldest, Lance, from Robyn's first marriage was thirteen, Andrew was ten and Nathan eight.

Meredith, as the only girl, was naturally the darling of the family. Her cousins doted on her, and her aunts and uncles showered her with attention. Nathan was the only one who seemed the slightest bit jealous, occasionally taking a toy from her or one-upping her with accounts of his accomplishments in school and listing the toys he'd received for Christmas.

Of course the children begged to open gifts first, so there was a flurry of ripping and crackling paper and a chorus of oohs and aahs as presents were revealed.

Charlie's parents treasured their wood gifts. Each of the children received something from their grandparents. Marian had wrapped a gift for Starla, as well, and though Starla knew the sachet and soaps were one of those gifts kept on hand for the last minute, she adored Marian for including her.

Marian opened a digital camera that Sean and Robyn had given her, and Sean showed her how to use it. "You can send us pictures in e-mail now," he said.

Immediately Marian had the children pose, and the adults were chased down next. She took a snap of Starla and Meredith looking at Meredith's new interactive alphabet game.

"Give me your e-mail address, and I'll send you these pictures," she said cheerfully and ran for a paper and pen.

Starla jotted down her e-mail address, and Marian continued with her picture taking until she claimed it was time to get dinner underway.

Charlie's sisters-in-law were gracious, including Starla in their tasks and conversation and showing genuine interest in her business venture in Maine. The women moved to the kitchen while the guys picked up the mess.

"You must have to fight the guys off with a stick," Donna said to Starla, "what with your looks and cooking skills."

Starla stirred the gravy she'd been assigned to tend. "I haven't had that problem so far."

"Well, I admire you for going after the career you wanted," she said sincerely. "You're still young and have plenty of time to marry when you're ready."

"Assuming she *wants* to marry," Robyn said. "She could be enjoying her independence too much to sacrifice it."

"It just hasn't been an issue," Starla said, stating the plain truth. "There hasn't been anyone I would have considered marrying. But I'm definitely not closed to the idea."

"You must be mighty selective," Donna said, "which is a good thing, because I'm certain that men will be lining up outside your restaurant just to get in and have a peek at you."

Starla felt her cheeks warm.

"You're embarrassing her," Marian said from the sink.

Donna finished brushing butter on a pan of rolls and slid them into the built-in oven. She moved over to where Starla stood at the cooktop. "Did I embarrass you? Jacob claims my mouth engages before my brain. I'm sorry."

Starla shrugged. "That's okay."

"I didn't mean any insult. I'd give anything to look half as good as you."

"I don't know what to say to that," Starla replied.

"Tell her to clam up while she's ahead," Robyn said.

They all laughed then and at the sound of Craig shouting for help, Robyn shot toward the door. "I'll bet one of mine has him in a headlock."

Starla's roast was a smashing success, along with the sweet potato soufflé she whipped together at the last minute. Both were complementary to Marian's turkey and stuffing, Donna's gelatin salad, and Robyn's green bean casserole.

Marian produced pumpkin and pecan pies along with a chocolate cream for the kids.

After dinner, Charlie helped his mom with the dishes, washing while she put away leftovers. Starla tried to help, but Charlie shooed her off. She was soon embroiled in an enthusiastic game of Monopoly with all five boys.

Meredith napped with her head in her aunt Robyn's lap. Starla watched as the young woman repeatedly threaded her fingers through Meredith's dark hair. Robyn glanced up. "I always wanted one of these," she said with a smile.

Charlie walked out of the kitchen just then. "You can borrow mine anytime you like."

He stood behind Craig and placed his hand on his nephew's shoulder. "Who's winning? Andrew, is that you with all the houses on Boardwalk and Park Place?"

Andrew nodded.

"If I land there once more, I'm done for," Starla told him.

On the next roll of the die, she did just that and gave all her money and property to Andrew before bowing out of the game.

Charlie found an open spot on one of the sofas and gestured for Starla to sit beside him. She wished she could lean into him, snuggle into his embrace or reach for his hand. Not touching him made her feel strangely empty.

Sean was talking about a situation at his job at an insurance company. Before long, the conversation shifted and he started telling tales about his brothers while they were growing up.

"Tell the one about when you hit Jacob's head through the tent with the baseball bat," Lance said. The boys had ended their game and came in to join the adults.

Without prompting, Sean got up as though he were about to give a performance. Starla knew why once she saw the moves that went along with his storytelling.

"I was walking along swinging my bat and saw the lump sticking out the back of the tent," Sean said, pretending he had a bat in his hand and swinging at the air. "I just gave it a *whack.*" To emphasize that word, he made a hitting motion with the invisible bat. "Mom screamed."

The others chuckled.

"I shot inside the tent and there was Jacob, knocked out cold. Mom didn't know what was wrong with him, but I did."

The boys all laughed and Jacob said, "Yeah, real funny."

Starla couldn't resist joining the laughter. Listening to their stories and jokes, she envied them their sense of family and their shared memories. They were close-knit, but not exclusive, because she was treated as a part of them. They held to tradition, but weren't too rigid to accept a guest and make her welcome.

Afternoon stretched into evening and the feelings of

acceptance and companionship only grew stronger. By the time night fell and Charlie's brothers and their families gathered gifts and coats and prepared to leave, Starla felt a loss at seeing them go.

After much kissing and hugging, they settled into their vehicles and Starla stood in the cold on the porch with Charlie and his parents, waving as everyone drove away. Charlie held Meredith in his arms and carried her back into the house. "We'd better get our things together, too."

Starla picked up a coffee mug and tray and carried them to the kitchen. Marian was wiping her eyes with her apron when Starla set the tray on the counter.

"Sorry," Charlie's mom said, flattening her apron over her waist. "I get a little weepy when everyone leaves. Having all the kids here reminds me of when mine were all at home. I miss my Kendra all the time, but terribly on days like this."

Starla didn't know what to say to comfort her. "She must have been very special."

Marian nodded. "She was our little darling, just like Meredith is now, doted upon, what with three brothers. But she never acted spoiled or took advantage of her position."

"Do you mind me asking how she died?"

"I'm glad to talk about her. People outside the family act like they don't want to bring up the subject around me for fear I'll go to pieces or something. And Charlie won't talk about her."

Starla nodded.

"She was killed in an auto accident on her way back

from town. She'd just gone for groceries. Meredith was with me that day, thank God. A truck crossed the center line and hit her head-on. She was killed instantly."

"That must be a small comfort."

Marian wiped her eyes again. "Thank you for asking about her."

It felt natural to take her hand. "You have a wonderful family."

Marian nodded. "Yes. I do." She smiled through her tears, then collected herself. "So, you'll be leaving tomorrow, dear?"

Starla's heart dipped at the reminder. "Yes. The tow truck is coming sometime in the morning. We should be on the road by noon at least."

"Well, it was a pleasure to have you here with us for Christmas," Marian told her and squeezed Starla's hand. "I'm so glad we got to meet you."

Starla gave her an impulsive hug. "I'm glad, too."

"Now, you know," Marian said, straightening and leading her back to the living room, "if you're ever through this way again, you have to stop by and see us."

Starla couldn't imagine a reason for her to be this way again, but she appreciated the woman's sincerity.

"I'll e-mail you those pictures."

"Thanks."

Charlie was waiting for her. Meredith hugged her grandparents, and the couple waved from the porch as Charlie drove them away.

Sitting in the passenger seat of the Cherokee, a feeling of loss and sadness swept over Starla so strongly that she fought back tears of her own and wondered if Marian was crying again.

Meredith kept up a constant chatter from the back seat, and Charlie replied occasionally. Starla thought of the gifts she received that day and knew she would treasure them as part of the memory of her stay with Charlie.

The log home welcomed them with the twinkling multicolored lights of the Christmas tree blinking in the great-room window. Charlie hit the garage door opener and pulled inside. Starla felt as though she was coming home.

But she was merely a visitor. And she'd be gone tomorrow.

"Can I take a bath in your tub with my new bubbles?" Meredith asked.

Starla could almost smell watermelon, and the remembered scent triggered a memory that made her heart skip a beat.

"Sure, then it's bedtime," her father said.

Starla put away the dishes she'd taken and watched the news while Charlie gave Meredith a bath. Cheeks pink and skin smelling like bubble gum, Meredith padded out in her new Power Puff Girl pajamas to give Starla a good-night hug.

"Night, sweetie," Starla said.

"This was the bestest Christmas," Meredith said. "Thank you for the Barbie."

"You're welcome. Thank you for the chest you made me."

"You can put your jew-lery in it and then when you get out your rings and stuff, you will memember us."

"I certainly will." Starla hugged her, wondering how people could bear it when they were separated from a child of their own through loss or divorce. Meredith wasn't her own and she was already feeling the deprivation.

She urged Meredith toward her room. "Sweet dreams."

Several minutes passed and she knew Charlie was reading a bedtime story. When he came out, he looked tired.

"Everything okay?" she asked.

He nodded.

"You have a great family. I had a really nice time today."

He took a seat beside her. "They liked you."

When Charlie moved his arm behind her shoulder, she was grateful to snuggle into his strength and warmth and feel the connection between them. *I'm going to miss you, Charlie. I'm going to miss this closeness and the way you hold me and touch me. I'm going to miss our talks and the way you smile and make me laugh. I'm going to miss everything about you and the new world I discovered here this Christmas.*

He picked up the remote and aimed it at the TV. "You watching this?"

She shook her head.

He jabbed the off button, sending the room into silence, and tossed the remote on the other end of the sofa.

This was it. Tonight was their goodbye, because tomorrow, when she carried out her things and made polite farewells, when the tow truck came for her, Meredith would be with them.

When Charlie lowered his head, she wrapped her arm around his neck and eagerly met his kiss.

Chapter Sixteen

The next morning Starla stood in the cold and squinted down the highway, a narrow stretch of ribbon in the three feet of snow that blanketed the countryside.

She'd carried her belongings to the Silver Angel, straightened the interior of the cab and retrieved her clipboard, fastening it to its holder on the dash. As she worked in the tilted cab, a speck of disappointment inched its way into her thoughts, but she dusted it away.

No use making herself miserable. No use dragging the whole thing out. She was an adult and she'd entered into a physical relationship with Charlie knowing exactly what she was doing, and choosing to do it because she wanted to.

The feelings that had crept in, feelings for Meredith, feelings for Charlie…that part had been unintentional and not of her own choice. But she'd known all along that she'd be leaving, and she was prepared for it when the rumble of a diesel engine reached her. In the distance, the enormous rig barreled down the highway.

Charlie had stayed with Meredith, so she trudged back to the house through the path in the snow, seeing tracks everywhere, prints of deer and rabbits, prints they'd made themselves when they'd traveled to the truck and across the yard on their search for a Christmas tree. Another snow or a few warm days and that evidence of her visit would be gone, too.

The lights on the tree twinkled from the window, raising memories best left buried. She opened the door and called in, "The truck's here! I'll be leaving as soon as he gets the Silver Angel out and hooked up."

Charlie bundled Meredith in her coat and hat and, after shrugging into his, carried his daughter outside.

"Can we see you driving your truck?" Meredith asked.

"I'm afraid not. The tow truck has to take it to a garage where the fuel can warm up before the engine will start. I'll be riding there with the driver."

"Maybe you can come back and see us," Meredith said.

Starla avoided Charlie's eyes, but looking into Meredith's was nearly as disturbing. "Maybe," she said lamely.

Meredith leaned forward and Starla hugged her. At the same time, Charlie's hand pressed the back of Starla's coat, tugging her toward them in a concealed embrace.

The enormous truck rumbled to a stop and the air brakes hissed. The driver got out.

"I had a wonderful Christmas with you," Starla said. "Thanks for everything."

Charlie's dark eyes hid his feelings, if there were any. Meredith stuck a finger in her mouth as though she was going to cry. Starla gave them a last trembling smile and walked toward the driver.

He had moved to the back of his rig where he was unrolling chain from a spool. It took a good thirty minutes to get the Silver Angel up on the road and securely hooked up for the tow to the garage. Charlie had taken Meredith back into the house and now he stepped out, his coat collar up around his neck. He raised a hand.

Seated in the passenger seat of the tow truck, Starla returned the gesture in a final goodbye. The wind ruffled Charlie's hair.

The driver released the brake and put the truck in gear. Within seconds they were on the highway, big wheels turning, carrying them away from Elmwood.

The CB radio squawked and a male voice spoke over the static, reporting a radar trap. The driver turned on his stereo, and a Garth Brooks song filled the cab. Starla had been in similar scenes so many times this felt like second nature. Everything was returning to normal—or would be as soon as she got the Silver Angel running, dropped this load in Nashville and returned the truck to her dad. She glanced in the rearview mirror and assured herself the truck was secure.

Getting her cell phone out of her bag, she called her restaurant's number. Geri answered the phone. "Hey, girlfriend."

"Starla! The tables and chairs are here! They're gorgeous! Wait till you see."

She'd missed the delivery, but compared to others, the disappointment was an easy one to absorb. "It will be good to get back. I'm on the road now."

Already her Christmas with the McGraws was in the past.

Starla sat at her desk in her office at the Hidden Treasure, her seafood grill in Beachtree, Maine, sifting through the mail and faxes that had arrived that day.

She paused, holding a fax from a prominent reviewer in Augusta, and read it over.

> Definitely a hidden treasure, located in an out-of-the-way warehouse district, this is the quintessential seafood and steak house in the area. Upscale, sophisticated, yet warm and cozy with a blackboard menu that changes daily. Staples you won't want to miss are the superb oysters, clam chowder, lobster bisque and tuna tartar. The pan-fried crab cakes are to die for, and the nut-crusted trout with ginger orange butter is a taste sensation. The excellent wine selection, comfortable atmosphere and friendly service are reason enough to make the drive. Simply the best seafood on the East Coast.

Making note of the newspaper in which the review was printed, she made a quick phone call, asking the acquaintance who sent her the fax to mail her the original article. She would frame the piece for the restaurant wall.

Taking the fax sheet, she carried it to her bulletin board and tacked it beside a colorful picture torn from a Barbie coloring book. She should be euphoric about the review. One of the most influential food critics on the coast had given her restaurant five stars.

Starla raised her hand and touched the colored picture beside it, remembering the little girl who had given it to her two months ago.

It was now the end of February.

Her vision blurred as she stared at the coloring. A now-familiar ache opened in her chest, and she placed her hand over it as though the pain was a tangible reminder she somehow appreciated.

On the pushpin holding the page was a pink plastic ring. Starla slipped it on her finger, and the familiar ache in her heart was like a bruise.

Her life had gone back to normal in the days and weeks after Christmas. She'd had the stitches removed from her forehead, and a faint pink scar was the only visible reminder of those few life-changing days. That and this picture…the ring…and a carved wooden box that sat on her dresser at home, drawing her attention and her touch every morning and evening.

Such a pitifully slim collection of mementos. No pictures except those developed on her heart. Marian had e-mailed her a few times, twice attaching photos. Starla had downloaded and saved them, but she'd never opened the snapshots. She knew what they were and she wouldn't subject herself to the pain of seeing them.

Sometimes she'd be working and glance up to see a dark-haired man entering the restaurant. At each instance her heart stopped. A hundred times she'd imagined Charlie finding her here, so the appearance of someone who resembled him nurtured that fantasy. But the man would turn so she could see his face, or a woman would walk up beside him, and the illusion burst.

Never Charlie. It would never be Charlie. She was foolish to allow the dream to perpetuate. Charlie had loved his wife, and no one would replace her.

Starla had never for a moment felt a lack of respect from him; to the contrary, he was almost reverent in his regard and treatment of her. What they had shared was mutual attraction and appreciation. But Charlie held part of himself in reserve. That part which had been only for his wife.

Starla admired him for his devotion. He was a man of integrity and sincere dedication. Kendra had been fortunate to have been loved by him, and Starla often wondered if the woman had appreciated the treasure she'd held: Charlie's heart.

"Starla, that's fantastic!"

She hadn't heard Geri come up behind her. When she turned, her pert-faced assistant manager was grinning ear to ear.

"Peter Austin gave us five stars! Oh my gosh! We've arrived!" She jumped up and down and impetuously hugged Starla.

"Yes, can you believe it?"

"I can, yes I can!" Geri released her. "We've worked so hard for this—*you've* worked so hard. Oh, Starla, what a triumph! Did you call your dad?"

"No, not yet. I just got the fax."

"Make me copies, so I can show everyone."

Starla removed the thumbtack, placed the paper in the copier and ran off half a dozen duplicates.

Geri took them. "We'll celebrate tonight, with lobster and that bottle of New Zealand sauvignon blanc I've been saving, what do you say?"

Starla nodded. "Okay."

Waving the copies, Geri danced out of the office, her dark hair swinging around her shoulders.

Starla replaced the fax on the bulletin board. Why wasn't she dancing like her friend? Her eyes were drawn once again to the coloring book page. Why did that silly thing suddenly hold more meaning than a review from Peter Austin? Maybe she should throw it away, erase that chapter of her life so she could move on.

She raised her hand to the page, but the ring on her finger caught her eye. Instead of removing the picture, she smoothed the paper and repositioned it with another thumbtack.

Maybe she would finally open those pictures she'd downloaded and face her feelings.

Maybe throwing herself into next week's menu was the safest thing she could do. Starla turned and found her tablet and pen.

That night they celebrated, but her heart wasn't in it.

"What happened at Christmas?" Geri asked in her quiet yet pointed way.

Geri had asked before. She and Starla had been friends since the first year of college, and she knew something wasn't right, but Starla hadn't wanted to share her confusion with anyone. This time when she brought it up, Starla couldn't hold back the words.

"I met a man."

Brown eyes wide, Geri set down her glass. "I knew it. That man with the daughter who stowed away in your truck. What's his name?"

She hadn't spoken it since she'd left all those weeks ago. "Charlie."

"What's he like?"

"He has a lot going on inside that he never lets on," she replied. "He's forthright, honest, loyal."

"What, no 'thrifty, brave and true'? You make him sound like a Boy Scout. What is he *like?*"

"He has eyes a dark-copper color. They're warm, but they hold a lot in reserve. His hair is dark and thick, silky to touch. His hands are strong enough to shape wood and work with tools, but gentle enough to tie a pigtail or..."

Geri leaned forward in her chair.

Starla raised a hand to the faint scar line on her forehead.

"You're killing me here," Geri said.

Starla looked at her friend and shrugged.

"You slept with him."

She nodded.

"He's not ready for a commitment."

"Oh, he's committed. But it's to his late wife's memory and to the child he had with her. I couldn't compete with that."

"You could compete with Jennifer Aniston and every female in the country for Brad Pitt. If you wanted him, he'd be yours."

"Geri, you know me better than that."

"Damn right I do. And I know that if you wanted him and told him you wanted him, he'd succumb."

"Succumb?"

"You are a prize, you just don't recognize it."

"Even if that was true, even if I pursued him—which I won't—I wouldn't want a relationship based on *succumbing*."

"I don't think that's a word."

"Geri, if I'd thought he wanted me I'd have been all over that man, well, more than I was, but he's still in love with his wife. You should see him when someone talks about her or when his daughter asks questions. It hurts him so much just to hear her name that he can't bear it."

"In other words..." Geri tapped her fingers on the tablecloth. "You can't play second fiddle to a ghost."

"Exactly."

"A ghost won't keep him warm at night."

"But she can keep his heart for as long as he lets her."

"Then he's an idiot. He could have you. Maybe someday he'll realize that."

Starla didn't hold much hope for that. He had never even asked for her phone number or her address. By now she was just a pleasant memory.

Meredith closed her angel book, got out of bed and crept to the window. It was summertime, but not so hot that the air conditioner was on yet, and she liked the sound of the frogs out her window. Sometimes when she and Daddy went for a walk by the creek in the daytime, frogs jumped from the weeds into the water. They didn't like to stay around people. But at night she heard them.

Angels were like that. Sometimes you got close to one but they didn't stay around people too much.

Daddy spent a lot more time with her now. But he was still sad a lot. He smiled and didn't want her to see his sad face, but she knew. First he missed Mommy. Gramma missed Mommy a lot, too, and she said that it was okay to be sad for a while. The person you missed would always be in your heart.

And now Daddy missed the angel lady. Meredith missed Starla, too. And she missed how happy Daddy had seemed at Christmas. She wished she had Starla's number so she could call her sometimes, but Daddy said he didn't know it.

In the pretty light from the moon, she could see Daddy. Sometimes when he thought she was asleeping, he went outside and stood like that, with the frogs making noise and the wind blowing his hair.

Overhead the sky twinkled with shiny bright stars, just

like the stars in *Pinocchio.* Meredith squeezed her eyes closed and wished on a star for an angel to bring her a new mommy and make her daddy not be sad anymore.

Crawling back into bed, she hugged her bunny and reached out to touch the Barbie Starla had given her. The doll slept on the pillow beside her at night sometimes.

The fairy made Pinocchio a real boy, so an angel could for sure bring her a mommy. She still believed.

Charlie pulled weeds away from his tomato plants and stood, the late-June sun hot on his bare shoulders. Meredith had gone to stay with Sean and Robyn for a week, and he missed her more every day. He was glad she was getting to play with the boys, and Robyn was probably spoiling her like crazy in the city, but her absence sure made the days and nights stretch out long and silent.

It gave him too much time to think, too much time to regret. Too much time to ponder his decisions and his life and the direction it was taking.

Life went on. That's all. Just as it always had. Life just happened. And he dealt with it as it came.

That was another of his flaws, never taking control and making life happen.

As his thoughts did all too often, they settled back on Starla. He admired her for a hundred reasons. She'd broken away from her father's expectations and forged a new life for herself. She hadn't gone along with the flow and ended up middle-aged and unhappy because she'd never taken the paddle and worked her way up a different stream than was expected. As he had.

Charlie had never cared enough to buck people's expectations. He'd been content to flow with the current, learn his craft, marry his childhood friend, sailing along placidly.

Even when his marriage to Kendra had soured, he'd thought it was honorable to stay married to her, raising his daughter, providing a home, even though he and his wife slept separately and neither of them seemed to care.

Why had he never jumped out of the boat and made his way to shore for a new start? He'd thought about it, but living up to his parents' expectations had been more important. He owed them, after all.

Charlie turned on the garden hose at the outdoor spigot, took a long drink that tasted like vinyl, wet his perspiring chest, then placed the hose and the flow of water at the base of his tomato plants.

And he *had* always believed there was a flaw in his character, because there *was* such a thing as love. He'd seen it between friends and family. His parents had been in love for thirty-odd years, his brothers had loving relationships with their wives.

He was the one who had never felt passion for a woman.

The sun beat mercilessly on his head and shoulders, searing a realization into his soul. *That wasn't true.* That was not true.

But if he admitted feeling the passion he had tamped

down, it would mean he had never loved his wife, because he'd never felt the same way about her. If he was completely and totally honest with himself, he would have to admit that he was not as brokenhearted as everyone thought he was. And somewhere in his barren black heart, he would unearth the ugly suspicion that his wife's death had been a...*relief.*

And for that ungodly thought, Charlie deserved to spend his life alone, unhappy, unfulfilled. The weight of his self-confession pressed on his physical body so hard that he dropped to his knees in the fertile black soil and felt the wet clods soak his worn jeans.

He'd been *relieved* when Kendra was no longer in his life.

Chapter Seventeen

A sound of anger and distress retched out of Charlie's soul and tore at his throat. He pounded his fist against the dirt.

The truth had been a secret so dark and so ugly that he'd buried it and been incapable of facing it. What kind of man felt a sense of freedom at the loss of human life? The loss of a good person, someone he loved, a woman his adopted family treasured and entrusted to him?

What kind of man was he?

An hour passed. Charlie's knees ached. His tomato plants were drowning. His shoulders were burnt from the sun. His throat was raw.

He was just a man. Not a bad one. Not an unfeeling one. Just a man who'd grown up as a lonely boy and felt indebted to the Phillipses.

Slowly he got to his feet.

He *had* grieved over Kendra. Just not the way everyone expected—the way he thought he should have.

And he could love. He'd loved his wife and he adored his daughter.

And he felt passion. He wanted Starla in a way he'd never experienced before and had been too guilt stricken to acknowledge. Admitting that he had fallen in love with her would have been admitting that he'd never had similar feelings for his wife.

And he hadn't been able to do that.

Not until this moment; when it was too late and Starla was long gone, living the life she'd chosen for herself.

God, how he admired her for that. Right now she was somewhere in Maine living her dream, cooking up lobster bisque, whatever the hell that was, and adding cumin to her soups.

Charlie glanced toward the creek, the frogs silent now in the daylight. The buzz of a bee met his ears, along with the distant rumble of a jet.

He'd moved out here to escape. Escape people and their expectations. But he'd heaped more of them on himself, unrealistic expectations sometimes. Like expecting to feel passion for a wife he'd never fallen in love with.

Looking out across his abundant garden and the waving grass and alfalfa that stretched over his acres, it was hard to remember the same land buried in three feet of glistening snow, the sky silent and gray. That's why it was such a good year for the farmers, because of all the snow. For every thing there was a season.

He loved Starla Richards, the ethereal beauty who had driven into his life one wintry night and changed everything. It wasn't Starla's fault that he hadn't felt the same for Kendra. It wasn't Kendra's fault, either. And he was sure, by God, finished blaming himself.

Some things just were.

Feeling as though he'd sweated off a hundred pounds that last hour, Charlie shut off the water and rolled up the hose.

He would shower, call Meredith, then go get himself something to eat in town. This epiphany stuff gave a man a hell of an appetite.

"Hey, Charlie!" Shirley called when she spotted him entering the air-conditioned interior of the Waggin' Tongue. "The little darlin' still off visiting Sean's family?"

He picked up a newspaper from the counter. "She'll be gone until the weekend."

"Must be mighty quiet out at your place."

He took a seat and she brought him a menu he didn't bother to open. "It's quiet all right. I'll have the hot beef sandwich on mashed potatoes with dark gravy and a side order of slaw."

"Coffee?"

"Milk and a glass of water, please."

"Comin' right up, sweetie."

He unfolded the paper and read the front page.

From the serving ledge on the window that separated the restaurant from the kitchen, Harry's stereo softly played an old Beatles classic.

Charlie'd been in here dozens of times since last winter, and he never failed to remember the heart-stopping fear of having his daughter missing or the following days that had changed him.

When the enormous silver rig with blue detailing rolled into the parking lot, it immediately caught his attention, and Charlie wasn't sure if he was imagining it or not. Just a similar truck, but lately everything made him think of her.

But no, there across the door was emblazoned the logo *Silver Angel* with the tilted halo over the *A*. Charlie's heart nearly stopped, then chugged so fast he thought it would burst from his chest. He laid down the paper.

The image of Starla stepping out of that truck into the snow, making her way to the door and inside the café, then shedding her coat took his breath away.

Still staring out the window, he got to his feet. Shirley was just carrying his drinks to the table, but he walked past her without looking and didn't see her curious gaze follow him.

Neither did he notice the heat that struck him when he opened the door and ran across the parking lot toward the truck.

The door opened and a jeans-clad leg and a boot appeared—a work boot. A *man's* work boot.

A man of about fifty with thick silver hair and mustache lowered himself to the ground and stared at Charlie. The stranger shut the cab door.

Feeling stupid, Charlie stared back. His gaze shot to the door again. This was the Silver Angel all right. His thoughts shifted to override the disappointment, and understanding reached his brain. Starla's dad. The Silver Angel was his rig. "You must be Starla's father."

The man smiled. Charlie noted he was tall and good-looking, and he could see where Starla had inherited part of her looks. "That I am. And you're…?"

Charlie extended a hand. "Charlie McGraw."

The other man had a strong callused handshake. "You're the man with the little daughter who has a big imagination."

"That's me. She's visiting my brother's family right now."

"Strange you being here like this. I was planning to look you up on my way through. I'm picking up a load of soybeans down the highway."

"I was just getting a bite to eat. Come on in and join me."

They walked to the café, boots crunching on the gravel drive, and Charlie held open the door.

Shirley kept Charlie's food hot until a plate was made up for the other man.

"I don't know your name," Charlie said when they both had a steaming plate in front of them.

"Vince."

"Starla thinks the world of you. She talked a lot about how close the two of you were while she was growing up."

"Yeah, she's my little Star. A beauty, that one, from the very moment she came into the world. Thinks for herself, she does."

Charlie nodded. A minute passed while they ate. "How is she?"

"She's doing great. Her restaurant is a big hit on the East Coast. Word is getting around, not to mention attention from some stellar reviews, and people are driving to Beachtree just to try the food."

Beachtree. Charlie hadn't known where she lived until that moment. Oh, he could have found out. His mom had Starla's e-mail address. He could have asked for it and written to her, asked where she lived, asked how she was doing…but he hadn't dared. He hadn't been able to deal with the flood of feelings that contacting her would unleash.

"What's it called, her restaurant?"

"The Hidden Treasure. She came up with that because it sounds piratelike and seafood is the specialty. The place is also out of the way, in a warehouse district. Clever, I thought."

Charlie nodded.

They finished their meals and Shirley brought slices of apple pie. "On the house," she said with a wink.

"You said you were going to look me up," Charlie said.

Vince Richards nodded. "I wanted to thank you for taking care of my girl. For sharing your family for the holiday and all. She appreciated it. I was relieved to know she was okay and that someone was looking out for her after she got that knock on the head."

"Did it leave a scar?"

"I hadn't paid attention, but she does wear her hair over that spot now. Hadn't thought about it, but maybe that's why. She's not a vain girl, my Starla. I always thought she could have turned out one of those stuck-up chicks nobody can stand. She has the looks, you know. Maybe it made a difference that we traveled all over and she was always the new kid in school. Leastwise I don't see her as uppity, maybe others see her differently."

"No," Charlie said quietly. "She's just as you describe her."

Shirley brought two cups of coffee and discreetly disappeared.

Vince stirred sugar into his. "She had a lot of nice things to say about you, too. I thought maybe the two of you would stay in touch, but I asked a while back and she said no."

Charlie's chest ached with the loss. He glanced out at the Silver Angel, sun glinting from her chrome smokestack and trim. "Can I be frank with you?"

Vince nodded. "I wish you would."

"I had a lot of crap to deal with. A lot of guilt over my wife and her death."

"You blamed yourself for her dying?"

"No. It's hard to explain."

"You don't owe me an explanation."

"I know. But I want to say something, and in order for it to make sense, I need to explain. I—" He looked at his cup, gathering his thoughts, then back at Starla's father. "I married my wife because it was expected. This is a small town, people make assumptions. Parents make assumptions, too. My parents took me in after my real mother died, and I felt indebted to them. My wife was their daughter and everyone expected us to get married."

"And so you did."

Charlie nodded. "Makes me sound gutless, doesn't it?"

"No. Makes you sound responsible. Kind probably."

"Yeah, well *kind* didn't make for much of a marriage. I shouldn't have married her for the wrong reasons. I cheated her out of something more."

"Least you didn't screw her 'cause she was the town beauty queen, knock her up and then have to make a marriage out of that mess."

"Personal experience?"

"We're talkin' man to man here, 'n' that's more than Starla needs to know."

"Sure."

"It turned out okay, I'm just saying people get married for a lot less honorable reasons than that."

Charlie looked into the man's blue eyes and read his understanding. He'd never spoken of this to another person and getting it off his chest felt right. "Anyway, what I was getting around to was that I didn't think I had a right to feel anything for your daughter. I didn't have anything to give."

"Now you do?"

That brought him up short. Maybe he did. "I didn't get her address or phone number because I didn't want to have them and argue with myself whether or not to use them. And I was afraid."

"Women put the fear of God in you, that's for sure."

"I don't even know...if there's someone else."

"All that and you could have just asked me if she had a boyfriend."

Charlie ran a hand down his face. And waited.

"Not that I know of."

"She would tell you?"

"She tells me pretty much everything. I didn't exactly get all the details about her time here with you, but she has her right to privacy."

Charlie felt his neck get warm.

Vince leaned to the side and reached into his back pocket.

"I'll get your dinner," Charlie said quickly.

"Thanks." He pulled out his wallet and unfolded a scrap of paper. "Got a pen?"

Charlie got up and fished a pen out of the cup beside the cash register. "Here."

On a napkin Vince copied an address and phone number, jotted down another number, then stuck the paper back into his wallet. He pushed the napkin across the table. "Don't waste too much time arguing with yourself. Life is short."

Charlie took the white napkin and stared at the numbers and street address. "I can't just call. What would I say?"

Vince chuckled. "I can't help you out there, boy."

What excuse did he have left? That she lived in

Maine and he lived in Iowa? Long-distance relationships had been known to work.

That she didn't feel anything for him? Their time together had been a romantic fling and nothing more? Could be, but he couldn't know for sure unless he stuck his neck out.

That he couldn't leave his daughter? It was summer vacation, and she was with Sean and Robyn for the rest of the week. If he asked, they would keep her longer.

"I'm going to go to Maine," he said.

Vince finished his coffee. "I wrote my phone number on there, too. I'd like to know how it turns out."

"You won't say anything about this?"

"Nope."

They stood and grasped hands.

"Thank you, Vince. For everything."

"I didn't do anything 'cept give you her address."

"You did more than that."

He paid and walked Vince out into the sunshine. The man got into his truck, and gravel crunched under the tires as the big rig pulled away. Charlie stood watching the taillights disappear down the highway. Then he turned and got into the Jeep. He had to get online and buy plane tickets.

Chapter Eighteen

Later the same night Charlie drove his rental car slowly past the Hidden Treasure restaurant. A neon sign with a treasure chest dripping jewels identified it. The interior was lit from within, revealing a considerable-size late-dinner crowd. Patrons filled the tables and a waitress carried a tray.

He imagined walking inside. She would be there, somewhere. But a public restaurant and her place of work wasn't the place to approach her.

Charlie drove to a stretch of moonlit beach and pulled out his cell phone to check on Meredith.

After speaking to her, he held the phone for a moment before shutting it off and placing it on the seat. He got out of the car and walked along the beach. He'd thought to wear loafers, thank goodness, so he slipped them off and carried them. The sand, still warm from the sun, felt good on his soles.

He was wired from the flight and he would never sleep tonight. He'd checked into a motel, but he couldn't wait. He had to see her tonight.

Loving Starla was the most unexpected thing he'd ever done. Coming here was the biggest risk he'd ever taken. He'd lived up to other people's expectations his whole life, and it was past time to do something for himself—just because it felt right and because it was what he wanted.

The breeze blowing across the ocean was cool and the air held a salty tang. The moon was a blue-white orb over the silvery water, the stars extending into eternity. What was a guy from the Midwest doing on a beach in Maine? He closed his eyes and listened to the roar of the surf. Foamy water curled around his ankles and soaked his pant legs. She loved it here.

After a childhood of driving the highways of America, she'd chosen this as her home, a place where seafood was plentiful and her restaurant could flourish.

If she *did* return his feelings, if there was any chance at all of them making something out of what they'd begun last Christmas, he could learn to love it here, too.

But how could he take Meredith away from his parents? So much for going after what he wanted, he scoffed at himself, but they were her only grandparents.

Could be it was just a dream, anyway. He didn't have to worry about it now.

Charlie walked along the beach, passing others

who were out for a stroll, occasionally pausing to sit on an outcropping of rock and watch the silver-crested waves.

He pushed the button on his watch to discover it was after ten. He'd checked the yellow pages and had seen that the Hidden Treasure closed at nine on weeknights.

Back at the car, he brushed off his feet and slipped them back into his shoes, then got in and drove to the address he'd memorized.

It was a small apartment building a few blocks from the beach, with a parking lot on the side. He parked across the street and stood away from the glare of a streetlight.

He didn't know what kind of car she drove. He didn't know her schedule. He just assumed that eventually he would see her or that he'd have the guts to knock on her door. If it was a security entrance, he'd have to identify himself.

Second thoughts about the wisdom of this trip plagued him. What if her father was wrong and there *was* a man? Just because they'd spent a few magical days and nights together didn't mean she felt squat for him. If she was in a relationship and he showed up, he could cause a problem for her.

Feminine laughter reached him, and he focused his attention on two women walking from the corner, carrying bags and grocery sacks. They approached the door of the apartment building and the light over the doorway shone down on pale blond hair. *Starla.*

Charlie's heart pounded with indecision. But one

thought stood out above all the others. No one would expect Charlie McGraw to do anything this impulsive. That woman was *his choice.*

The fact gave him confidence and propelled him across the street and up onto the pavement near the door. Both women whirled in surprise at the sound of him running toward them.

An expression of concern and mistrust immediately crossed the dark-haired one's face.

The other, Starla, wore an expression of amazed recognition. She shifted the bag in her arms.

"Sorry, I didn't mean to startle you," he said.

"What do you wa—" the dark-haired woman started to say, but Starla interrupted.

"Charlie?"

He took a few steps closer and nodded.

"What are you doing here?"

"Well..." His face warmed. He glanced at her companion in embarrassment. "I was in town..."

Starla's friend spoke up then. "I forgot something I have to do this evening. I'll call you later."

Starla gave her a grateful smile and a hug. "Thanks, Geri."

After watching the young woman walk away, she turned her full attention on Charlie. "You weren't in Beachtree, Maine. What are you up to? Is Meredith all right?"

"She's fine." He jammed his hands into his pockets and admitted, "No, I wasn't in town. I came to see you."

Starla seemed to collect herself. She found her keys

and let Charlie take the grocery bag while she unlocked the door and led the way into the building.

He followed her up a flight of stairs and waited for her to unlock another door. In her apartment, she turned on lights. She wore a sleeveless top and a soft flowing skirt with sandals, revealing golden tanned limbs, an ankle bracelet and a toe ring. Her silver blond hair was fastened back on both sides in a girlish style.

Charlie glanced around, realizing how little he knew about this near-stranger. Her furniture was typical cottage style, with floral prints and a mixture of white wicker and old painted wood. He could see her living in a beach house one day.

She had the life she wanted. Whenever she'd spoken of Maine and her restaurant, he had envied her the excitement in her voice. He was a country boy with a child to raise and a penchant for cheeseburgers and fries. What had he hoped she'd ever see in him?

"I'm surprised to see you," she said.

"I'm surprised to be here."

"How did you find me?"

"I saw your dad. He stopped at the Waggin' Tongue when he was picking up a load of soybeans."

"He didn't say anything."

"I asked him not to."

"Oh." She gestured to her plump floral sofa. "Have a seat. I'll make us something to drink. What would you like?"

He shook his head. "Nothing."

"Well, I need a minute in the kitchen alone." She left

the room and he heard water run. A minute later, the microwave dinged. She appeared with two mugs and sat one in front of him on the low wicker table. "It's tea."

He remembered she didn't drink coffee at night. But they'd shared a bottle of wine more than once.... His heart hitched into overdrive. He raised the mug to his lips and looked at her over the top of it.

She perched on a nearby chair. "So Meredith's fine, you said?"

"She's with Sean and Robyn. They went to Adventureland today."

"I get an e-mail from your mom occasionally."

His mom had never said anything.

A clocked ticked nearby, and Charlie glanced over to see a mock fireplace in distressed white wood. Inside the opening was a candelabra designed from driftwood. Shiny rocks and shells were scattered around it. "You have a nice place."

Starla had picked up her mug, but she set it down without taking a drink. Her heart felt as though she had run all the way home from work. Twice. Seeing Charlie had been such a surprise, a wonderful surprise, but this awkwardness that buffered them made her uncomfortable.

He'd come to see her! She placed a hand to her breast.

He wasn't saying anything. Her eyes stung and she blinked.

He looked so good. Tan and strong and his dark hair was clipped shorter than when she'd been at his home. He wore an ivory button-down shirt that emphasized his dark coloring and broad shoulders, and a pair of tan trousers. She'd never seen him in anything but jeans…and, well, *nothing*.

Her heart flip-flopped at that racy thought and the vivid memory. Charlie naked. Yes, that was impossible to forget.

"We could discuss the weather," she said. "I assume you flew in, so I could ask about your flight. I don't have to be anywhere until tomorrow morning."

It was meant to be a teasing remark, but Charlie got the point because the next thing he said was, "Do you have someone?"

She blinked, uncertain of his meaning.

"A boyfriend? A lover?"

Well, that was certainly direct. "No," she answered softly.

"Is there any chance," he began, "that you could feel something for me?"

There it was, that rush of hope she'd tamped down for safety's sake. She couldn't take having her hopes raised, not when the chances of having what she really wanted were so slim. It took all her courage to say, "I feel something for you, Charlie, that was never in question."

His dark eyes brimmed with passion and uncertainty. He moved from the sofa to where she sat and knelt before her. Quite naturally, she reached out and laid her hand against his face, loving the well-remembered feel of his warm skin against her palm.

He turned his face and pressed his lips against the skin, and that easily lit the fire inside her.

"I felt something for you from the very first," she admitted.

"More than desire?"

It was a risky question. One that deserved a risky answer. "You had the love of your life, Charlie," she admitted. "I could never have hoped to compare to that."

Those dark lashes came down over his eyes for a moment, and when he opened them again, she could see the regret. She was right not to hope, because he couldn't love her the way she needed. He still loved his wife.

"And I'm a selfish woman. I don't want to play second fiddle to a memory."

Charlie made a sound then, something he turned into an uncomfortable clearing of his throat. When he reached up and took her hand away from his face and reached for her other hand, his strong fingers were trembling.

"I want to tell you something. I'm afraid of what you'll think of me, but it can't be worse than what I've thought of myself for all these years."

"I'm listening, Charlie."

And she was...with her whole heart.

And so he poured out his feelings about his wife, purged himself of the guilt and regret, all the while exposing his vulnerabilities and admitting his weaknesses.

Starla listened, her heart aching for the misery he'd lived with. And as he talked, hope took root and blossomed inside her. She understood now, understood why he'd been so reluctant to talk about Kendra, why he'd clammed up and refused to share with her. All this had been festering on the inside of him.

He wasn't pining for his dead wife.

And he'd felt guilty because of it.

"You're not a bad person," she assured him.

"I know that now. I just couldn't get past it all or learn to deal with it until I met you. What I felt for you right away was so different, I was scared. It made everything else glaringly wrong. And I couldn't admit that."

"You didn't do anything wrong," she told him. "You did the best you knew how."

"I want to promise that I can make things work out for us, but I still don't know how."

"Nothing in life is guaranteed."

"We're so different, you and I."

"Not all that different."

"I live on a country road in the middle of alfalfa and cornfields. You live near a beach and hear the foghorns at night."

"That's just where we're living, not who we are."

"Maybe it is."

She pulled her hands from his and framed his face. "It's not. *This* is who we are."

And with that, she leaned forward and kissed him as she'd been dreaming of for the past six months.

Charlie wrapped his arms around her and pulled her forward so that she slid from her chair to the floor, and they clung to each other, Charlie's hand pulling her against him and sculpting her bottom through her skirt.

She kissed him until she was dizzy with wanting

him and deliriously happy at having him close. She pulled away enough to say, "I've missed you."

"I've missed you, too, Starla. I love you."

She cried against his lips, earnestly trying to control her emotions enough to get out the words to express her own feelings. "Cha-arlie," she managed.

"Say it again."

"Charlie. I love you, Charlie." And remembering what she'd heard him say to his daughter so many times, added, "With my whole heart."

He buried his face in her hair and hugged her so tightly she could barely breathe.

She couldn't get close enough to express what she needed. After pulling his head down for another breathtaking kiss, she used his shoulders as a balance to push herself to her feet. She took his hand and urged him up.

He followed her to her bedroom, where she didn't turn on any lights. The light spilling through the blinds was enough to illuminate Charlie's face and hair.

In record time, she had peeled off her clothing and started on his, a difficult task, because he touched everywhere she bared and pressed kisses to her skin. He pushed her back onto the bed and lowered himself over her.

"I didn't bring anything with me, I didn't plan—"

"It's okay, it's a safe time." She urged him with her hands and body and he groaned when he entered her.

It was like the first time. It was like starting over. Their coupling was tender and urgent, sweet and yet daring—sweet because it had been so long, daring because they could give everything this time.

Afterward they lay wrapped in each other's arms, her head on his shoulder. "How is this going to work?" he asked, a dilemma on his heart still.

"You and me? I thought we had it down pretty good."

"I mean how can we be together? I've thought about it, and nothing I have is as important as you—except Meredith, of course. I can leave it behind and not look back, but I don't know how to take her away from my folks."

She propped her chin on the back of her hands on his chest and looked at him. "What *are* you talking about?"

"Aw, damn," he said and sat up quickly. "I'm such an ass." He took her hand and kissed it. "Starla, will you marry me?"

She got up on her knees and leaned forward to kiss him. "Yes."

They smiled into each other's eyes in the semidarkness.

"But I would never let you take Meredith away from your family. They're important to her—and to you."

"Then how—"

"That's a no-brainer, Charlie. I'll move to Elmwood. I love your home."

"But your restaurant. That's your dream, and you'd have to leave it behind. You worked hard for it."

"You're right, I did, and I love the place. But nothing about it has given me as much satisfaction as being your wife will. Ever since the opening, there's been a hole inside me, a place where you belong.

"I can sell it or I can keep ownership and let Geri and the staff run it. It wasn't just the Hidden Treasure that was my goal. It was a place of my own, a place to call home and feel like I belonged. I felt like I belonged at your place, with you and among your family. That's what I really dream of."

"You'll miss the work. The cooking."

She thought a minute. "I can always open a place in Elmwood."

"But the seafood is here."

"True. But there are refrigerated trucks." She smiled. "And I can always experiment with corn."

He laughed then. "You'd be happy as an Iowa girl?"

"I'll be happy as your wife. And Meredith's stepmother."

He hugged her. "She will be ecstatic."

"Let's call her."

He pushed her down onto the bed and nuzzled her cheek, kissed her lips. "Let's wait till morning."

Epilogue

Meredith overturned a box of toys and scrambled through the dollhouse furniture and Little People in search of her Christmas book. It would be Christmas in a few more weeks and she hadn't read it for a long time.

It wasn't on her shelf with her other books, and it wasn't under her bed. It had to be here.

She sat down on the floor, and a cardboard box in the corner caught her eye. Some of her things were packed up, ready to move. As soon as her new room upstairs was finished being painted pink, she would move up there and have a bigger room with a big-girl bed. Her old room would be for the new baby.

She opened the box and there on top was the Christmas angel book. She opened it and looked at the familiar pictures. Daddy and her new mommy, Starla, still said Starla wasn't a real angel. But Meredith knew better. Ever since Daddy had married her and Starla had come to live with them, Daddy was happy. So happy he smiled and laughed and sometimes he even told her about her first mommy when she didn't even ask.

Daddy said it was okay to miss her, and that they would always love her. But he said it was okay to start to forget her sometimes, too. It didn't mean they didn't love her so much, it just meant she had been gone a long time and real people were easier to think about than gone people.

Starla said Daddy's smiles were special because they came from way inside and it had taken a long time for them to find a way out.

Daddy said Starla's smiles lit up the sky better than the moon or fireworks or anything.

They were funny sometimes.

And they both said Meredith was the smartest, prettiest girl ever. But they also said that they had loved her first and that even when the new baby came, she would still be their special girl. They would just have two girls to love then, 'cause the baby in Starla's tummy was a girl, too.

Meredith closed the book and carried it with her to find Daddy and her new mommy. They were in the kitchen, tasting something Starla was cooking, and Daddy was licking it from her fingers.

"What are you making?"

Starla wiped her hands on a towel and smiled. "A cake."

"The one with the chocolate chips?"

"The very one you love."

"I might have to eat some ice cream with that."

Daddy picked her up and set her on a stool at the counter. "What've you got there?"

"My angel book. Will you read it to me?"

Daddy sat beside her and read the book. He took his time and used the voices he used when he pretended he was the people in the stories. She loved to hear her daddy read. Almost as much as she loved to hear him laugh.

He got to the last page and looked at the picture of the family. "Look, Star."

Starla looked at the picture, too. Then they looked at each other.

There was a daddy and a mommy and two little girls, just like always. Why did they look at it funny all of a sudden?

Starla came around the counter and stood where she could wrap her arms around them both. Daddy hugged her and Meredith.

"It's going to be a very special Christmas this year," Daddy said.

"Meredith," Starla said, "I think we're going to find an angel for the top of the tree."

Meredith squealed with delight.

"Are you sure we need to do that?" Daddy asked.

"Why not?" Meredith and Starla chorused together.

"Well, because I've already got my two angels right here."

The three of them laughed.

* * * * *

If you enjoyed what you just read,
then we've got an offer you can't resist!
Take 2 bestselling
love stories FREE!
Plus get a FREE surprise gift!

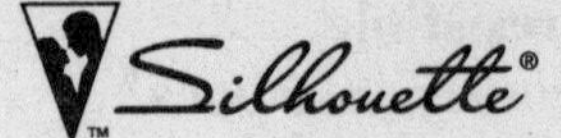

SPECIAL EDITION®

COMING NEXT MONTH

#1633 HOME ON THE RANCH—Allison Leigh
Men of the Double S
Rancher Cage Buchanan would do anything to help his child—even if it meant enlisting the aid of his enemy's daughter. Beautiful Belle Day could no more ignore Cage's plea for help than she could deny the passion that smoldered between them. But could a long-buried secret undermine the happiness they'd found in each other's arms?

#1634 THE RICH MAN'S SON—Judy Duarte
The Parks Empire
After prodigal heir Rowan Parks suffered a motorcycle accident, single mom Luanne Brown took him in and tended to his wounds. Bridled emotion soon led to unleashed love, but there was one hitch: he couldn't remember his past—and she couldn't forget hers….

#1635 THE BABY THEY BOTH LOVED—Nikki Benjamin
When writer Simon Gilmore discovered a son he never knew was his, he had to fight the child's legal guardian, green-eyed waitress Kit Davenport, for custody. Initially enemies, soon Simon and Kit started to see each other in a new light. Would the baby they both loved lead to one loving family?

#1636 A FATHER'S SACRIFICE—Karen Sandler
After years of battling his darkest demons, Jameson O'Connell discovered that Nina Russo had mothered his chid. The world-weary town outcast never forgot the passionate night that they shared and was determined to be a father to his son…but could his years of excruciating personal sacrifice finally earn him the love of his life?

#1637 A TEXAS TALE—Judith Lyons
Rancher Tate McCade's mission was to get Crissy Albreit back to the ranch her father wanted her to have. Not only did Tate's brown-eyed assurance tempt Crissy back to the ranch she so despised, but pretty soon he had her tempted into something more…to be in his arms forever.

#1638 HER KIND OF COWBOY—Pat Warren
Jesse Calder had left Abby Martin with a promise to return… but that had been five years ago. Now, the lies between them may be more than Abby can forgive—even with the spark still burning. Especially since this single mom is guarding a secret of her own: a little girl with eyes an all-too-familiar shade of Calder blue…

SSECNM0804